MW01690640

KINDNESS, CLOSE CALLS, AND THE MAGIC OF MAKING WISHES COME TRUE

WISH MAN

FRANK SHANKWITZ

CREATOR & A FOUNDER OF MAKE-A-WISH® FOUNDATION

WISH MAN

© Frank Shankwitz. 2018. ALL RIGHTS RESERVED.
Authored by Frank Shankwitz

Published by TitleTown Publishing
Green Bay, WI
www.titletownpublishing.com

No part of this book may be reproduced in any form or by any means, electronic or mechanical, including photocopying, recording, taping, or by any storage and retrieval system, without the written permission of Frank Shankwitz or TitleTown Publishing.

Interior design by Euan Monaghan
Cover design by Travis J. Vanden Heuvel
Cover photo © TitleTown Publishing. ALL RIGHTS RESERVED

ISBN (hardcover): 978-1-949042-09-2
ISBN (paperback): 978-1-949042-08-5
This title is also available in electronic and audiobook formats.

PUBLISHER'S CATALOGING-IN-PUBLICATION DATA
Shankwitz, Frank
WISH MAN / Shankwitz
1st edition. Green Bay, WI: TitleTown Publishing, c2018.

Proudly Printed in the United States of America
10 9 8 7 6 5 4 3 2 1

Dedication

To my wife Kathleen Carlisle Shankwitz, who found me when I needed to be found, believed in me and my ideas and goals, and supported both. She supported my career as a police officer, which often consisted of late-night call-outs and weeks away from home during investigations. That takes a special kind of persona and love. Thank you, Kathleen.

Acknowledgements

To Juan Delgadillo of Seligman, Arizona, who became my father figure when I was 10 years old because my father was 1,800 miles away. Juan taught me how to take care of myself, a work ethic, integrity, honesty, respect, how to develop a positive character, introduced me to both sports and music, and, most importantly, how to give back.

To the Polk and Ortega families of Seligman, Arizona, who took me in and provided a place to live and meals when there was nothing.

To my teachers and coaches at Prescott High School, who helped me through high school, making sure I was always on the straight and narrow.

To Clay Smith, the manager of the Safeway Store in Prescott, Arizona, who employed me all throughout high school, and always adjusted my work schedule so I could attend football practice, games and special high school events.

To my stepmother, Elinor Shankwitz, who loved me like I was her own son, and taught me the graces and how to be a gentleman.

To the United States Air Force, who completed the transformation from boy to man.

To Daphine, an off-duty emergency room nurse who wouldn't give up and brought me back to life when I was pronounced dead.

To Colonel Ralph Milstead, Director of the Arizona Department of Public Safety, who supported my idea of founding the Make-A-Wish Foundation and allowed me to shift adjust to accomplish the mission.

To Scott, Kathy, Alan and Linda, the co-founders of the Make-A-Wish Foundation, who helped make it all happen.

To the thousands of staff, volunteers, sponsors and supporters of the Make-A-Wish Foundation who accepted my idea, supported it and made it grow.

To the Wish Children – God Bless them all.

To my daughters, Christine and Denise, for their love and gifts of grandchildren and great-grandchildren.

To Allyn Reid, publisher at Sherpa Press, who suggested this book and has spent countless hours editing.

To Clarissa Burt, who introduced me to the people that would open a whole new career path in my life.

And finally, to Gregory Scott Reid, who in my senior years, became my mentor, and more importantly, my friend, who has made things possible in my life that I never imagined possible.

Contents

Foreword

In 1980, there was a young boy, by the name of Chris, who was living out his final days after being diagnosed with childhood leukemia. Chris had one dying wish: to be a Highway Patrol Officer, and with the help of the local community, and the Arizona Highway Patrol, his wish came true. What happened that day, and in the days to follow, was truly magical and is difficult to put into words.

Part of the team helping to make that young man's wish come true was none other than Frank Shankwitz, the creator and a founder of the Make-A-Wish Foundation. Frank realized something tremendous when he helped to fulfill that first wish—he could change the world through simple acts of kindness. With that realization, Frank decided he wanted to start a non-profit foundation that would let children 'make a wish' and have it come true. The Make-A-Wish Foundation came to life, and today it is one of the largest, and most well-known, children's charities in the world.

What I've learned from Frank is that perhaps there is no major task staring us down each day as we try to tackle our life's purpose. What if it was simpler than that? What if small acts of kindness were the actual key to our impact on the world? With what started as one small wish, Frank found a way to help children realize their dreams, before it was too late.

In 1980, there is no way Frank could have known how his role, in that one event, could cause ripples so large, they would be felt and talked about around the world. When Frank participated in fulfilling that first wish, he forever changed that child's life, and his own, accidentally. With wishes, he and his foundation have put magic and hope in the lives of children who, in their darkest moments, are in dire need of that light and that love.

Through the Make-A-Wish Foundation, Frank has had the opportunity to create ripples so great there will never be a way to fully comprehend how many lives he has touched. Life has a funny way of letting us forget how important it is to use each day to enrich the world around us. It isn't easy to focus on leading a meaningful life, a passionate life, but it is necessary if your wish is to make an impact and leave a legacy.

Our purpose is our impact. We have all been tasked with leaving the world better than we found it, and we do this through the ripples we make, and the lives we change. Every single day is an opportunity to change a life. Let Frank show you how your life can be a gift to the world around you through simple acts of kindness. With each chapter your will feel your heart and soul come to life as you realize the impact you can make.

Remember … one small wish started it all.

—GREG S. REID

Introduction

Every life is a journey. Every aspect of our lives, from birth until death, influences our ultimate destination. That destination may or may not be our original goal, but I have come to believe that the journey always takes us where we are supposed to be, even if we didn't know we wanted to be there. As a child, I followed my mother as we trekked across the country to a different life and lifestyle than I'd ever known. It was her dream, not mine, but it led me to people and places that shaped who and what I am today.

Every child has a dream. They want to grow up to be a cowboy, a doctor, a lawyer, a teacher, or a firefighter. Some want to be nurses, singers, artists, and mommies or daddies. Every birthday marks an opportunity for a new dream or wish—some wish for ponies, baby dolls, or bikes. Others wish for simpler things, like food or clothing. Still others wish for something so profound and life changing that even adults cannot contemplate being in their shoes.

As a young boy, my greatest wish was survival. My childhood was much different than many boys', but similar to some. I dreamed of food and shelter, better days and easier times, when I didn't have to wonder where my next meal was coming from or labor for it. It was my childhood struggles that led me to dream of a stable, secure future for me and my family.

Today, I am grateful for my childhood. While it wasn't easy, I learned how to work hard and be self-sufficient. Most important, though, it led me to a forty-year career in law enforcement—another step on my journey that introduced me to people who had a lasting imprint on my life, especially children. Throughout my career, I availed myself of the opportunity to visit schools, where I taught children bicycle safety and volunteered as a coach for Special Olympics programs. These endeavors were rewarding and a way for me to use my career to make a contribution to the lives of others. I had achieved my dream—my wish—or so I thought.

Then I met Chris. Only seven years old, Chris was on his own special journey, and he had a wish—a wish so profound that it could not, should not, go unfulfilled. Since I helped to grant his wish, hundreds of thousands of children have also had their greatest wish granted, and my life's journey has been forever changed. Before then, it was enough for me to be a dad, a cowboy, and a highway patrol officer. But meeting Chris changed all of that, and his impact on my life has changed my destination. It wasn't a place I knew I wanted to be . . . but it is exactly where I know I am supposed to be.

Everyone has a unique journey. I invite you to walk with me through mine as I share the events, people, and places that made me the person I am today. I am a cowboy. I am an Arizona Highway Patrol officer. I am Frank Shankwitz—the Wish Man.

Chapter One
On the Move

The trip was uneventful, if you don't count the hours spent replenishing water in the radiator and driving aimlessly from one wrong turn into another. I sat in the front passenger seat of our Jeep Willy station wagon for what seemed an eternity for a ten-year-old, while my mother, Lorraine, moved us from Michigan to Arizona. In reality, the trip took several weeks—we'd drive for a while until we were low on gas and food money, then Mom would get a waitressing job in a small town just long enough to put some cash in her pocket and gas in the tank before heading west once again. During the entire trip, I tried to imagine where we were going, expecting to see a lot of cowboys and Indians, horses, and the stuff Western movies were made of. But I had no idea what to expect; truthfully, I didn't even know where Arizona was—I just knew that my mom wanted nothing more than to be there . . . and I did not.

I was staring out the window, wondering where we were and how much longer it would take for us to get there, when it happened. The sun disappeared and the blue sky turned an eerie shade of green before grayness took over and turned to black. Not knowing what was happening, the panic in my mother's voice was frightening enough—even before I saw the raging twister.

"Oh, God. What do I do? What do I do?" she mumbled as she peered out the windshield over the top of the steering wheel. As the funnel took shape and its tip threatened to kiss the highway, the still air was overcome with dust and debris.

"What do I do!" she screamed, no longer able to hold her composure.

Frozen, I instinctively gripped the seat and held my breath, helpless against the monster that was about to overtake us. Then, suddenly, Mom jerked the car over to the shoulder and slammed on the brakes.

"What do I . . . What do I . . ." Desperation set in as she fumbled for the door handle and swung open the door. Not knowing what else to do, I followed suit, wishing my hands would stop shaking so I could escape. The rain which had begun just minutes earlier had turned to hail, balls of ice that stung as they pelted my skin as I ran to my mom, whose red hair was standing straight up into the dark sky. A quick glance around and I could see we weren't alone—cars and trucks were haphazardly parked along the highway and their occupants were scrambling out onto the road—appearing as helpless and uncertain of what to do as we were.

"Get in the culvert!" a trucker shouted as he jumped from the cab of his truck, motioning with his arm for us to follow him as he ducked his head and took off running. Mom grabbed my hand, and in a split second, we were running after him with supernatural speed. It seemed like my feet hardly touched the ground as we jumped down a bank and crawled into a big cement tube that ran under the road. More than a dozen of us stayed there, watching with horror through the opening as the tornado roared over our heads. Curled into a ball with my arms wrapped around my knees, I cried, not knowing what was happening, but knowing I'd never been so terrified in my life. Then suddenly, as if someone had turned a switch off, it grew quiet, and Mom squeezed my shoulder.

"Thank God that's over," she sighed. "C'mon, let's get going."

As we retraced the steps back to our car, much slower this time, the sun reappeared, as if nothing had happened. But the trees, uprooted and thrown to the ground, told a different tale of destruction and the sheer force of Mother Nature. However, because the tornado had gone just to the side of us, but not directly over us, there was no damage to the cars lining the sides of the road. Regardless, I wasn't going to forget, and at that moment I decided that long car trips weren't for me. Still unable to talk, I didn't say a word—I didn't have to, but Mom knew what I was thinking.

"It's all right, sweetie. We're okay now," she said.

Her words of encouragement had little effect. I didn't want to be there. I didn't trust the road; I didn't trust the sky, knowing that could be deceiving and could change in an instant. My eyes were glued ahead of me, intently peering out the windshield, searching for a sign of another twister and a place to go if another one should pop up. Mom could see my fear and must have figured she needed to cheer me up and take my mind off of what had just happened, so she pulled over at the first small store and ran inside. When she came out, she was carrying a cowboy hat—a real, authentic cowboy hat, which she plopped on my head with a smile. I gave her what she wanted—a smile, weak and uncertain as it was—and once again, we went down the road.

Finally, we reached the Arizona border, where an inspection officer stopped us, took a look at our old green station wagon, which was loaded on top and inside with everything we owned, and ordered, "Unpack it."

Quick on her feet, my mother replied ever so sweetly, "I'll be glad to unpack it if you'll pack it all back up." Her tactic worked, and the officer waved us through with a resigned, "Get going."

We had arrived in Arizona but were still not at our destination, which was Williams—the town my mother had uprooted us to and one she said we would call home. The sun had set and night had fallen before we reached the outskirts of the town, and with nowhere to go, nowhere to stay, and no money to stay there if we wanted to, Mom found a spot of flat land for us to set up shelter. Surrounded by trees and plush forest, it provided us with the perfect clearing to set up our beds at night. Well, they weren't really beds, but rather bedrolls which we laid on the ground next to our station wagon. With all our moving from place to place, Mom had gotten quite skilled at packing our Jeep, making sure the things we needed first and most often were readily accessible. She kept our bedding at the very back, making it easy for us to get them out at night and put them back in during the day.

This little spot of earth and our station wagon, faded green, accented by rust and dents, became our temporary home. Neither were anything to write home about—if I had a home, that is. These days, people would say we were homeless, and they would have been right. But Mom tried to make it an adventure, calling it camping.

It was our home for the night, and it was a far cry from Michigan.

Chapter Two
Chasing Someone Else's Dream

I was born in the Windy City, where my mother was born in 1920. She rarely talked about her childhood, but from pictures, it appeared her family was successful. Her father was a banker, and they lived in a very nice house in a good neighborhood. In every photograph, my mom and her brother, Earle, were clean and very well dressed. For some reason, though, Mom didn't get along with her father and refused to share details about her childhood with me. Her feelings were so strong that she made sure I really never got a chance to know her dad or spend any time with him.

Mom also didn't like city life. She preferred the country and absolutely loved the summers she spend at an aunt and uncle's farm in Iowa, where she took to farm life like it was second nature. She and Earle cared for the livestock, feeding the cows, pigs, horses, and chickens, and helped harvest the crops in the field. Both became accomplished horse riders, a passion they carried with them throughout their adult life.

But it was the cowboy life, not the farm life, that attracted her. She was enamored with the West and everything about it. In her teens, she read about Fred Harvey and the Harvey Houses he'd built along the Santa Fe Railroad, from Los Angeles to Chicago, and dreamed of being a Harvey Girl. Harvey Girls were the name given to the waitresses who worked in these fancy restaurants, serving elegant meals to the trains' passengers. Longing to leave Chicago and experience the world on a grander scale, especially the West, she applied for the prestigious position, knowing she could be assigned anywhere between home and California. Her assignment took her to Williams, Arizona, a small town west of Flagstaff that sits on the historic old Route 66. In fact, it was the last town to bypass the legendary cross-country route.

Before she applied to be a Harvey Girl, my mother dated my father, Frank. However, when she moved, her world broadened. It was 1938 and Mom found herself embroiled in the cowboy way of life. It was everything she imagined—the gateway to the Grand Canyon, Williams was a small mountain town surrounded by authentic western ranches. She fell head over heels in love with cowboy life, working as a Harvey Girl in Williams, with the bonus of relieving vacationing "girls" in Winslow, Ash Fork, Seligman, and the Grand Canyon. During her time there, she became involved with the people and even donated her time, collecting clothing for the Catholic Church to send to needy Native Americans on the nearby reservation. She also fell in love with a genuine cowboy—a young man from a local ranch—and they made plans to one day marry. Those plans changed in 1940, when my mother received word that her mom was dying from cancer.

When she returned to Chicago to take care of her mother during her final months, my grandmother made a final request—she wanted my mom to get back together with Frank and to marry him before she died. Despite her deep infatuation with western life and the love she had left behind, my mother agreed and complied with her last request.

It should come as no surprise that the marriage wouldn't last. My father and Chicago, Illinois, were everything that Williams, Arizona, was not. Chicago was populated and devoid of ranches, livestock, and anything cowboy. Hot, humid summers were the setting for city kids to play in blocks of bungalow houses set in a row, and the winters were frigid, leaving traces of dirty snow. It was a stark difference to the snow-capped mountains and high pines in Williams that mirrored the scenic background portrayed on traditional Christmas cards. My father, Frank, was also the farthest thing one could get from a cowboy. Employed by Montgomery Ward, he worked in the catalog production department. After they married, my mom got a job working on the production line of the Seeburg Jukebox Company, which transformed into an aircraft parts plant during World War II, making Norton Bomb Sights. My father tried to enlist in the military during the war but was rejected due to a heart murmur. By all appearances, they were a typical young married couple, working to make something of themselves and build a life together.

In 1943, I joined the family, although it had probably already become troubled by that time. By the time I was a toddler, around the age of two or three, my mother left and I went to live with my dad's parents. I don't remember being upset about her absence, though. In reality, the memories I do have were good—we had many fun family times together with my dad's sister, Bernice, and her family. She and her husband, Bill, were my favorite aunt and uncle. I was surrounded by laughter, wonderful pork chop dinners, and cousins who took to me to cowboy movies and bought me treats.

Naturally, I was too young to have any real sense of time and have no idea how long my mom was gone. At some point, though, she did return.

Once again, though, the reunion was short lived. My parents were just too different to be happy together, and my mom obviously had difficulty being a traditional wife. When I was in kindergarten, they divorced and the next phase of my life began. My mother was given custody of me. The divorce decree stipulated that custody of me went to my mother as long as she stayed in the greater Chicago area—should she leave the area, custody would revert to my father. Always the rebel, my mother grabbed me and left the city, saying we were moving to Arizona. I was far too young to have any sense of direction, but she took an unusual route, heading north to Michigan, near the Green Bay area, where she had friends. This is where I got my first taste of roughing it. We lived in a camping tent in a state park next to Lake Michigan, and Mom got a job in Cedar River. While she worked, I was left alone to fend for myself. There weren't any kids to play with, but the beaches and shores of the lake served as a big playground. There also weren't many amenities—an outhouse served as my toilet and the lake was my bathtub. A peanut butter and jelly sandwich was my usual lunch—at least for a while, until there wasn't enough money to buy food. It was only then that I can recall being hungry or needing anything.

One day during that summer, my father surprised me by arriving at our camp while my mom was at work. Having spent the entire summer trying to locate us, he grabbed the few clothes and things I owned and told me we were going back to Chicago. Boy, was I excited to see him! I remember being happy during the entire trip, and even happier when he stopped and bought me a big hamburger and some new, clean clothes. When we arrived, I got settled into his apartment, which was really nice and more than a little different from sleeping in a tent.

I settled back into city life, adjusting easily. I had clean sheets, clothes, and hot cooked meals three times a day. Dad enrolled me in school, and I was enjoying having playmates. Then one day while playing at recess, someone suddenly grabbed my arm and said, "Let's go." I turned my head and there stood my mother, who told me she'd moved back to Chicago and now had a job and an apartment, where I'd be living with her. Confused to say the least, I did as I was told and got in the car, which took us to a not-so-nice apartment in a rundown part of the city. Again, I was enrolled in a new school and had to make new friends; however, because my mom worked the 4:00 p.m. to midnight shift and the neighborhood wasn't very desirable, I wasn't allowed to go outside or play with anyone after school.

From there, the back and forth continued, my parents continually warring over who would raise me. I was on the playground at school the next time my dad showed up. He spent a few minutes talking to my teacher and then took me home to live with him. My mother found me a few months later and once again grabbed me off the school playground, this time telling me we were moving to Michigan, where she had a new job. It was becoming so very confusing, but I was too young to truly understand what was going on or argue about it.

Our new home was an old farmhouse outside of South Haven, Michigan. There were no kids around to play with, but at least this house had running water and a bathroom. Mom told me we would be staying there for a short time—just a couple of months—until she had enough money for us to move to Arizona. Not surprisingly, a couple months turned into a few years. Again, I adjusted nicely. I was able to keep myself occupied and only had two problems: food, or the lack thereof, was always an issue, and I missed my dad and had no way to contact him.

Of course, we didn't have a telephone—we also didn't have TV or even a radio. We relied on an electric wall heater that was supposed to heat the whole house. The kitchen had an electric stove and a wood burning kitchen stove which were our backup when the electricity went out in the winter, which happened regularly in Michigan's cold, harsh winters. The cold winter nights also led to awakening many mornings to find that the pipes had frozen. This, too, occurred so often that my mother always kept a large pan of water on the stove, ready to heat, when the pipes froze shut.

Our house was an old two bedroom, one bath farmhouse that Mom rented. It was located at the end of a dirt road, surrounded by farm fields and apple orchards. At best, one could say it was shabby. Lacking any curb appeal whatsoever, the white paint on the exterior was old and faded, and the front door was nailed shut because of wood rot on the front steps. Our entrance into the house was at the rear door, which had a small covered porch. The furniture came with the house and rested on bare wood floors surrounded by walls covered with wallpaper that had been peeling for some time. We didn't have much—just the bare necessities: an old couch, a rocking chair, an end table, a coffee table, a small kitchen table with three chairs, and a bed and dresser in my mother's bedroom.

My bed consisted of an Army surplus cot. I used an old fruit crate for a nightstand, and more fruit crates, stacked on top of each other, became a makeshift dresser. I had several blankets and comforters to keep me warm in the winter, but it was miserable getting out of bed in the morning. Even when the electricity wasn't out, the house felt cold and drafty, and I never wanted to get out from under the warmth of the covers, knowing I'd be shivering in the cold while getting dressed.

Also on the land was a small barn, which was as old as the house, and half of the building had fallen in before we moved into the house. However, we were able to raise chickens in the part that was still standing. An old threshing machine had been deserted by a previous occupant and sat outside the barn and served as my toy—with a good imagination, I pretended it was an Army tank, a bomber, or a train engine, whatever I was in the mood for at the time.

By anyone's account, we didn't have much, but Mom made use of what we did have. Mom was willing to accept the shabbiness of our house and sparse furnishing, but she was a clean freak and kept the inside neat and tidy. In the summer, she took advantage of the rich Michigan dirt and planted a small garden where we grew vegetables to eat. I also picked apples from the nearby orchards, and she would make pies and applesauce. In the summer, there was always something to eat. The winters, however, were a much different story.

The closest farmhouse was about a half mile away, and it was in even worse shape than ours, if that's possible. There weren't any kids my age around, so I spent most days by myself, exploring and wandering down the road to other farms. That's how I landed my first "job."

Because I was big for my age, a local farmer taught me how to drive a tractor during the fall harvest and paid me fifty cents to pull a large wagon while the farmers pitched hay onto it. It was a good deal, the best part being getting fed lunch by the farmers' wives. They'd bring a big basket out to the field, and we each got two sandwiches and lemonade. Harvest lasted a month, and that lunch was my big deal every day, leaving me well-fed at the end, with more than a dollar and a half in my pocket.

School started again, and I was enrolled in a school in South Haven instead of the rural school most of the farm kids attended. It was a mile from our house to the bus stop, and I walked it every day. Michigan winters can be brutal, and walking a mile in the snow back and forth to school might seem just as brutal, but the truth is I liked rural life and the solitary time spent walking past the fields. It was even more bearable after one of the neighboring farmers gave me an old, but warm, winter coat, hat, and rubber boots to wear. Apparently, the neighbors had noticed and taken pity on our living conditions and financial situation.

A young boy walking a mile to the bus stop certainly attracted attention, and the bus driver was no exception. Also the janitor at the rural school, the school bus driver struck me a deal: If I would be at the bus stop at six thirty in the morning, he'd pick me up and take me to the rural school, where I was to start a fire in the wood stove and get the school warm before the kids arrived. In return, I'd get a couple muffins, fresh baked by his wife every morning, and a thermos of hot cocoa. After he picked up the rural kids and brought them to school, I got back on the bus and he'd complete his route, picking up the town kids and taking them to school. Once I was at school, I received a free lunch, which I later learned was the reason my mother insisted I go to school in town. Having breakfast and lunch five days a week was great, but dinners in our house were few and far between. There simply wasn't enough money.

In early spring, I had a surprise visitor—my father. When he saw our living conditions and my lack of decent clothes, he was shocked and insisted that I was going back home with him. This time, though, I didn't. We had a long father-to-son talk. I told him how much I missed him, but that I really didn't want to live in Chicago. I truly liked the farm and my life there; the only things I missed were him and having friends my age nearby. Even more surprising than the visit was the fact that my parents listened to what I had to say and actually worked out a deal together. Every other week during the summer, I'd catch a train that stopped in South Haven and went directly to Chicago and would spend the weekend with my dad. For the first time since their divorce, I actually had a visitation schedule and would be able to see both of my parents!

This arrangement worked very well, and it ended up being a very special summer. My dad had enjoyed some success at Montgomery Ward and moved up the ladder. He had a very nice apartment and was dating a lady just as nice. Elinor treated me well, though I believe when she first met me, she was more than a little shocked by my appearance. Tactfully, she suggested they would get me a haircut and take me shopping for some new clothes and shoes. I met Marc, her son from her first marriage, who was a few years younger than me, and we all got along fine. During my visits, I got to spend time with my dad, which I thoroughly enjoyed, and I had the pleasure of being fed well by Elinor and being her student as she taught me manners and how to be polite to adults and ladies.

In the middle of the summer, my mother received a surprise package—a beautiful handcrafted Navajo rug, sent to her as a thank-you from the Navajo reservation in Arizona for the work she'd done years before collecting clothes for their people. As she hugged the rug and admired its intricate detail, her desire to live out West was renewed and she vowed right then and there that we were moving to Arizona. Just a couple weeks later, after returning to Michigan from visitation with my father, my mother quickly packed all of our belongings in the car, saying we were moving to Arizona. Again, I was confused—I thought my parents had come to an agreement that worked for everyone. I knew it worked well for me. But my mom insisted that my dad wanted to take me back to Chicago, and if we were in Arizona, he wouldn't be able to find us. I tried to tell her I didn't want to go. She wouldn't hear it, and once again, I was uprooted, leaving everything and everyone behind—even my dog, Corky, a black lab who had been my only playmate in Michigan. Corky chased our tail lights until he couldn't run anymore, and I cried until I couldn't cry anymore.

My mom was chasing a dream, our dog was chasing us, and I was wishing I could run as far away as I could. We were on our way to Arizona—a place where my mother really wanted to be, but the last place I wanted to be. I didn't care anymore if I was in Michigan or Chicago—just as long as I wasn't with my mother.

Mom and me on the horses

Dad and Elinor sharing a dance

Chapter Three
Juan

We were in the mountains, and it was getting colder. My mom explained to me that the elevation was seven thousand feet and because it was fall, it might even snow. She told me to hurry and gather some wood so we could make a fire and stay warm, and as soon as we had a nice fire burning, a light drifting snow began to fall. We quickly got the tent out of the car, and just as we were setting it up, the top ripped, leaving behind a gaping hole. It must have been the last straw for my mother, because she started crying, a loud, helpless cry that scared me. Pulling herself together, she admitted to me that we only had a couple slices of bread left to eat and the car was almost out of gas. We had no money, and it was snowing and there was a hole in our tent. At this point, most people would have admitted defeat, but not my mom—she told me to gather some more wood for the fire.

Usually, I listened to my mom, and I knew this wasn't a good time to argue. I walked through the pines trees and edge of the forest, gathering as much wood as I could. There wasn't much else I could do, but at least we'd have a fire. The mood was subdued as we went about setting up camp, but the quiet was interrupted by a heavy rumble. As it grew closer, I could feel the pounding of the earth before I saw its source. Then suddenly, a cowboy on a horse emerged from the forest into the clearing.

Tipping his hat at my mother, the cowboy winked at me and said, "Howdy, folks. I'm Herman Polk and you're on my ranch. I saw the smoke and need to know what you're doing here."

"I'm so sorry," my mother said. "I didn't know this land belonged to anybody. We were just planning to stay here until I found some work."

As the cowboy took in our "campground," torn tent and all, and my mother's red and swollen eyes, he sat down with my mom and asked her to tell him what was really going on. Giving in, she put her usual pride aside and explained our plight, and when she was done, the cowboy told her to sit tight. He was going to go home and get his truck and bring us back some gas for the Jeep so we could drive to his ranch house, where we'd be staying for the night. To me, he was like a savior—a cowboy sent from heaven.

A short while later, Mr. Polk returned with a five-gallon gas can. True to his word, he put some gas in our car and told my mother to follow him to the ranch house, where his wife, May, was waiting for us. I was excited, but even more so when I walked into the ranch house and felt the warmth from the fireplace and smelled the food cooking in the kitchen. A nice hot meal after all of those weeks living on peanut butter and jelly sandwiches made all of our traveling worth it.

While we waited for May to finish cooking dinner, Herman asked him if I could help him put the horse up in the barn. An authentic cowboy, he treated me very nicely, and I wanted to help him if I could. After I told him I was ten years old, he said I was pretty big for my age and he thought I could handle taking the saddle off of his horse and carrying it to the tack room. Never having been around a horse, I was nervous, but Herman showed me how to approach the horse and told me to rub it, not pat it. Then he helped me properly remove the saddle and made sure I could handle carrying it to the tack room. The whole time I was grinning from ear to ear—I was actually being a real cowboy.

When I returned from the tack room, he showed me how to rub down and brush the horse, explaining that brushing helps remove any burrs or stickers. "Don't want a horse with a burr under the saddle. Won't make for a happy day," he said. It was one of many lessons shared by him that have stayed with me forever.

Mom had been helping May in the kitchen when we walked back in, and the food smelled absolutely wonderful. I beamed with pride when Herman announced, "I hope there's some good grub; this young man just earned his dinner." And there was. I don't think I looked up from my plate one time—I just kept eating the juiciest and most delicious steak and baked potatoes I'd ever tasted, while Herman and May listened to my mom share her adventures as a Harvey Girl and our trek there from the Midwest.

As our stomachs filled and we were finally content, Herman told us about his brother, Tommy, who lived in a small town about an hour or so away called Seligman. "His wife, Thelma, works as a maid at the Supai Motel, and she might be able to help you get a job," he explained. It was perfect—my mom really needed to find work, and cleaning was definitely her forte. Herman talked to his brother and learned that there was an opening, and told us that if my mom got the job, Tommy would let us stay at their house until we found a place to stay.

"The best of luck to you both," Herman said as he walked us out to our car the next morning. After saying our goodbyes and thanking them for their kindness, we set out on the road again, taking the old Route 66 into Seligman. The trip would only take an hour—the shortest jaunt we'd taken since leaving Michigan. Mom remembered the town from her days as a Harvey Girl, and we had no trouble finding the motel.

When we arrived, a lady walked out and greeted us. "You

must be Lorraine and Frankie. I'm Thelma Polk, Tommy's wife. Tommy is Herman's brother."

Mom was introduced to the owner and hired on the spot. She had a job and would start the next day. Thelma said she'd be off work in just a few minutes and then we could follow her to their house.

The Polks lived in a small house on the edge of town, close to the grade school and high school. The kitchen and living room were one big room, similar to today's great rooms, but smaller, and that's where we'd be sleeping. Thelma matter-of-factly explained that we'd be staying there until we got on our feet and then asked my mom to help her get supper started—Tommy would be home from work soon. On the menu was biscuits and gravy, which I quickly learned was Thelma's specialty for both breakfast and dinner. You didn't hear any complaints from me—I was thrilled to eat, and warm biscuits and gravy twice a day was fine by me.

We were introduced to Tommy when he came home from working for the Santa Fe Railroad, and he immediately asked me to help him in the barn, saying his brother, Herman, had told him that I was a good worker. My job would be to clean the stalls and help him feed and water the animals. He was really nice and said to let him know if I needed anything and ask any questions I wanted. I liked my job, especially on cold mornings, because when I got done, I'd go into the warm kitchen, where my breakfast of biscuits and gravy would be waiting.

I was immediately enrolled in grade school and found I was as much a novelty to my classmates as they were to me. Most of the students were Mexican and Native American, with only a handful of white kids. I had never been around Mexicans and Native Americans before, so to me, they were unusual. However, because I was one of the few white students, big for my age, and had bright red hair and freckles, I definitely stood out from the rest of the class. I took a lot of teasing from the other kids because I looked so different, but they didn't mess with me. My size probably helped me there.

Living with the Polks wasn't bad. They had two sons of their own—Joe, who was still in diapers, and Robert, who was about six. Mom and Thelma worked at the motel, and I did my chores in the barn. After a while, Tom introduced me to the Santa Fe station master, who gave me another job. When the trains stopped to change crews, the new crew would have to haul ice to the engines and fill the water coolers. However, nobody was too keen about the job, so they'd pay the kids in town a nickel to haul the ice for them. There were some days when I'd make as much as a dollar a day hauling ice.

Tom showed me around the railroad, explaining that it was a division point, meaning the freight and passenger trains would stop there to change crews and add steam locomotives before heading eastbound over the mountains, or remove the locomotives from the westbound trains that had just come from the mountains. He gave me a tour, showing me the roundhouse used to turn the locomotives, the steam plant, repair shops, and the large stockyard with loading ramps that were used to load cattle from ranches before they were shipped east. Most of the men in the town worked for the railroad, and the railroad allowed the boys in town to use the showers in the locker room whenever they wanted, day or night. I soon became one of the cleanest kids in town, taking advantage of all the hot water I could ever ask for.

I liked Seligman and developed an appreciation for nature that was inspired by the beautiful scenery. Yellow land would stretch for miles, finally meeting low, rolling hills. The sun shone brightly throughout the day, producing glorious sunsets in shades of gold and plum before settling into darkness. It was a simple town with a simple life, but that's all I'd ever known. In Seligman, I was just like the rest of the kids, other than my appearance, that is. Like the other kids, I also found a job to help support my family.

That job was at the White House Café. They'd just fired their dishwasher, and Tom mentioned my name as a fill in until they could find a replacement. My mom took me to the café, and though I was only ten, they hired me, saying I could work there until they could find someone else. In the end, I worked there for four years. It was my first real hourly, paying job. I earned sixty cents an hour and one free meal a day. On school days, I worked from six to eight thirty in the morning, then I'd go to school and return at the end of the school day, when I'd work from three thirty until seven or eight at night.

Most of my time at the café was spent standing on my toes—even though I was tall for my age, I could barely reach the dishes that piled around the sink. A high-pressure sprayer and conveyer belt made it easier to clean the dishes, but pots and pans weren't so easy. Some were nearly half my size. In order to remove the food that had stuck to them, I had to use a steel brush and copper scrubbing pad, as well as a lot of elbow grease. The biggest obstacle to overcome was the short-order cooks, who were a dime a dozen and seemed to change more often than the seasons. Most were fired for being drunk or drinking on the job. Despite their intoxication level, though, they were demanding about having clean pots and pans available at all times. If there was even the slightest hint of anything that resembled food stuck to one, they'd lean down and get within inches of my face and the yelling would begin.

"C'mon, little baby, learn how to clean this shit right!" That's what I could understand; I had no idea what they were screaming in Spanish, but I imagined it was worse. To be honest, the cooks scared me, so I tried to work faster and harder, never standing up for myself or doing anything that might make them any angrier.

Over time, though, I became more interested in cooking than dishwashing. I paid attention to the cooks, watching them as they prepared meals from scratch. When I had the nerve, I'd ask them if I could help. One morning, the cook disappeared and the owner couldn't find him. I did, though—he was passed out over a sack of potatoes in the back room. The owner told me to cook the hash browns, eggs, bacon, and hotcakes that day. I can only imagine their reaction if the customers knew that such a young boy was cooking their breakfast for them.

The money I earned at the café was turned over to my mother to help us get on our feet—Mom was saving it so we could get a place of our own. My spending money came from hauling ice at the railroad. After living with the Polks for a couple months, Tom announced that he had found us an old travel trailer that my mother could get cheap. A 1940 twenty-eight-foot travel trailer, it had a small shower, a fold-out couch, and a piece of plywood attached to a chain that pulled down for use as a table. It needed repairs, but Tom volunteered to help get it in shape. He repaired cabinets, fixed the sink and toilet, and replaced its propane heater with an electric heater; he was even generous enough to let us keep the trailer on his land. However, because we were tied into the Polks' electricity and had no hookup for bathroom waste, Tom made a deal for my mother to park the trailer on the road behind the motel where she worked. We were able to run water and sewer lines to the trailer, but we couldn't afford enough propane to take hot showers, so Mom used the motel showers and I continued to use the showers at the railroad. The trailer was my home from that time until I graduated from high school.

One evening after working the night shift at the White Horse Café, I walked out the door and stood under the awning, watching a dark-skinned man who had been laboring for a few months, busy pounding scraps of lumber together. He was under the scaffolding when I crossed the street, curious about what he was building.

"Hi, I'm Frank. Who are you?"

Without flinching, he replied, "I'm Juan. Grab a hammer."

The man sounded serious, but I noticed the lines around his eyes crinkle before his lips turned upward into a bright and friendly smile. I'd done chores on the farm, worked at the café and the railroad, but I was still a young boy and had no idea what to do with a hammer; but I took the hammer he extended to me.

"Help me finish this place, and I'll cook you one of the first hamburgers," he said.

Watching Juan and admiring his skill for joining boards together, I swung the hammer hard, missing the head of the nail a few times before I got it. After that, I spent many days with Juan, swinging the hammer and doing what he asked as I helped him build what would eventually become one of the most famous stops on Route 66—the Snow Cap diner.

In time, a few of my friends joined me, helping Juan whenever we could. Although the school in Seligman had a lot of students, very few actually lived in town. Most lived on ranches outside of town or on the Indian reservation in Peach Springs. The handful who lived in town became my friends, and Luke, Chuy, Pat, and I spent that summer hanging out and working with Juan. Once the last nail was pounded and everything was painted, it was opening day for the Snow Cap, and Juan was true to his word—the four of us boys got to eat his first cheeseburgers. They were amazing, and one of the reasons the Snow Cap became such a popular attraction.

Juan Delgadillo was in his late thirties when I met him in 1953. He was a muscular man with black hair, but what I remember most about him were his laugh lines—not wrinkles, but real deep and evident laugh lines like cat whiskers that fanned out from the corners of his eyes and mouth. He was a hard worker but always had time to brighten someone's day. He also always had time for me, taking me under his wing and sharing his knowledge about everything from cooking to life lessons. One day, Juan said he wanted to make me something, but I had to let him know if I liked it. He opened the metal lid of the ice cream freezer and plopped the largest scoop of vanilla ice cream I'd ever seen into a glass. I watched, fascinated, as he poured creamy brown root beer over the top. Then, he pulled out a handheld silver mixer and put it in the middle, and the ice cream and root beer spun together into a delightful, creamy concoction. When Juan handed me the glass, I didn't know if I should eat it or drink it, but he gave me the answer when he put a straw in his own glass and took a sip. Following suit, I also took a sip—small and cautious at first—and found the fizz, sweetness, and coldness of the mixture unlike anything I'd ever tasted. It was beyond delicious, so much so that all I could manage to say was "mmmm."

That was all Juan needed to hear. "You love it! Great!" he exclaimed. Satisfied that his creation had earned my approval, Juan began making root beer freezes for his customers, and they quickly became another restaurant favorite.

But it wasn't just the food that made Snow Cap famous—it was Juan's sincere love for people and his unique character that made it one of Route 66's most loved historic places to visit. I continued to work there after the diner opened—my payment being one of Juan's big juicy burgers—and I loved witnessing Juan as he interacted with his customers. In the five years I worked there, I came to enjoy my time at the Snow Cap not only for the food, but for the entertainment. Juan was a prankster and loved to have fun with his patrons—from the moment they figured out which of the two doorknobs actually opened the front door, I'd watch as he pulled tricks from his sleeve, one after another. Sometimes I'd stick around when I was done working, just to see what he'd do next.

One night, a couple who had been on the road all day stopped in for a late-night snack. I waited with anticipation as I watched them try to open the door and give each other a subsequent smirk when they figured out the doorknob prank. As they walked inside, Juan untied his apron and tossed his spatula aside to hurry around the counter, where he stared seriously and intently at the couple as they looked at the menu, reading "Cheeseburgers with Cheese," "Hamburgers without Ham," and "Dead Chicken Sandwich." They chose the specialty. "We'd like two cheeseburgers and ..."

Before they could finish, Juan interjected. "Would you like those raw or cooked?"

"Uh, cooked, pl..."

Juan threw his head back and laughed—a big, roaring laugh exaggerated with both hands holding onto his stomach. It was enough for the couple to realize the game—Juan was teasing.

"We'd also like two Cokes and an order of fries," the man said. "Oh, and can we have some ketchup for the fries?" his wife added.

It was Juan's opening. He reached under the counter and pulled out a red plastic bottle and squeezed it. Anticipating ketchup, the woman instinctively jumped back to avoid being squirted, only to realize that it was red string that was spouting from the bottle's tip. Quite proud of his antics, Juan let out another huge laugh, while I sat on the freezer, watching the entertainment and keeping my lips pursed around the straw in my root beer freeze to keep myself from laughing out loud.

"Do you need some napkins?"

"Yes, please," was the reply, and Juan responded, reaching down and grabbing a wad of napkins—covered with ketchup, mustard, and lipstick stains. The couple looked at each other, obviously a bit unsettled to be offered such a mess. After a moment of hesitation, Juan said, "Ohhhh, you wanted clean napkins?" The mood lightened as the couple laughed, knowing now that the pranks were part of the ambiance of the diner.

As Juan prepared their food, I knew I should go home, but I was pretty sure there was more to come and didn't want to miss the encore Juan had planned. I stuck around, hoping they would order dessert. I patiently waited, and while Juan prepared their order, the couple moved to a table outside. Juan and I both jumped up to the counter when the woman walked back in.

"Can I have a couple straws, please?"

Juan obliged, placing a couple bundles of real straw on the counter. Quickly getting it, she smiled and rolled her eyes before asking for *real* straws, this time.

We waited until they finished eating and were tickled when they ordered dessert.

"We'd like two ice cream cones, please," the man said.

"Coming right up," Juan replied, as he retrieved two cones, which were no larger than the size of a person's thumb. Adding the tiniest scoop of ice cream to the top, he reached over to hand them their cones. "That'll be three dollars each."

They crossed their arms, smiling, by now, enjoying the show as much as I was. Juan took one look at them, acting confused, then looked down at the cones and said, "Oooooh, you wanted the *large* cones."

For the first time, I laughed right along with them. This is what it was like working with Juan every day. I thoroughly enjoyed my time working at the Snow Cap, and Juan became a good friend and role model in my life.

It wasn't all work in Seligman, though. Kids will be kids, and I was no different. My friends and I were always looking for a new adventure. Most kids my age had play train sets, but I was lucky—I had the real thing to play with. Getting to know the men in town who worked for the Santa Fe Railroad, I was allowed to hang around the roundhouse, watching as the men turned the big engines and locomotives around. What a thrill it was when they let me operate the levers that turned the track! In the train yard, they also let me pull the handle that switched the tracks. Really, it was a boy's dream come true. Sometimes, they would let me help drive the switch engine that would line up the cattle cars at the stockyard pens, or let me have the fun of riding on the small hand pump work cart they rode on to check tracks. I remember a couple of times when freight trains derailed just outside of town, and I got a firsthand view. Front row and center, I rode the work train and watched the huge equipment they used to replace the railroad ties and tracks and then put the undamaged train cars back on the track.

Being a spectator also provided entertainment. Anything new and different was considered exciting in small town life, but it was unexpectedly the government that provided us with excitement for a few years. Between 1951 and 1958, and again in 1961, the U.S. government

SNOW CAP - Seligman, AZ

Juan Delgadillo - SNOW CAP

conducted nuclear bomb testing outside of Las Vegas, Nevada. When the dates and times of the tests were announced, it was a big event in Seligman. Many people in the town would load up into the beds of pickup trucks and take a dirt road to the top of a high mesa just west of town, where the phone company had installed a relay tower. The top of the mesa provided us with a clear view to the west. Even though Las Vegas is approximately 180 miles west of Seligman, when the bomb blasts occurred, we could clearly view the glow in the sky from the bomb. At the time, it was an incredible sight. I should point out that we could not see the much touted mushroom cloud. When the blasts occurred, radiation from the nuclear bombs blew from west to east, right over towns in northern Arizona, including Seligman and Prescott. However, we were assured by the government that there was no danger to the people living in the path of the radiation. Watching the blasts provided us with entertainment and something to talk about. But memories of the excitement were replaced with regret in later years. It was while I was in high school that several adults and some classmates in both Seligman and Prescott died from cancer-related illnesses. It wasn't until the late 1990s that the U.S. government admitted the nuclear testing from the 50s and 1961 was the cause of cancer-related illnesses to residents of Nevada, northern Arizona, and southwestern Utah. As a result, the government authorized the affected "Downwinders" compensation in the amount of $50,000. My mother was one of those affected, and I was able to obtain the $50,000 in compensation for her a couple of years before she died, which allowed her freedom from worry about medical bills or other financial issues in her last years.

Little did we know our "entertainment" of watching the bomb blasts would later kill so many. But it was part of growing up in Arizona, just one of the many memories I've carried with me throughout my lifetime. Those years molded me, gave me my work ethic, and introduced friendships that I treasured both then and now. I loved my life out west and the people in it. We didn't have much money, and a hot meal at home wasn't common, but I'd found a way to make money and managed to get a meal when I needed one. Not only was I surviving, but I'd built relationships that had a huge impact on my life.

The only thing I really missed was seeing my father.

Chapter Four
Finding My Place

Two of my grade school classmates lived in town and one lived on a ranch on the outskirts. Jesse, a Mexican who went by the nickname "Chuy," lived with his parents and brothers and sisters in a railroad boxcar that had been converted into a home. His dad, like so many in the Seligman area, worked at the Santa Fe Railroad, and his mom worked with my mom as a maid at the Supri Motel. Over the years, our families became friends, and my mother and I enjoyed many of Chuy's mother's homemade beans and tortillas for our evening meals. Chuy was the one who gave me the nickname "Pancho," which means Frank in Spanish. The name stuck throughout my adult years.

Another friend, Luke, was a Zuni Indian. His family lived in a small shack by the railroad tracks, but we rarely spent time there because it was just too small. Luke had developed the artistic talent of many Native Americans and often spent time creating pencil drawings of the surrounding mesas, which he sometimes sold to the railroad crews for a quarter. Luke taught me to draw, as well, and I was pretty good, but never developed my talent when I grew up.

Pat was my only white friend, and he lived at the Diamond A Ranch headquarters just outside of town. He was also the only friend who didn't have a paying job in town—his job was doing chores at the ranch. I often went to the ranch and helped him carry out his chores, and in return for caring for the horses and calves, I learned how to ride—bareback because I didn't have a saddle—and I also got a free meal. Pat's father would often say I'd worked a man's day and had earned a man's dinner. It always filled me with pride when he said that, and I won't deny that I was very thankful for the many meals I had in their kitchen.

Not surprising since he lived on a ranch, Pat competed in the junior rodeo in saddle bronc and steer riding. Pat talked me into steer riding, and when we had a chance, I practiced riding, without rigging, on their steers. I wanted to enter the rodeo, too, but I didn't have the three-dollar entry fee for steer riding. When Juan learned that I need three dollars to enter, he let me work at the Snow Cap after hours, mopping and cleaning up the outside to earn the money. I entered several rodeos, riding to surrounding towns with Pat in the back of his parents' pickup truck. I had big dreams of being a rodeo cowboy, but those dreams quickly faded in my first rodeo, where I saw that the steers were about twice the size of those I'd practiced on.

Needless to say, I was inexperienced and ill-equipped to ride those steers, and I knew it. I competed anyway, making two qualifying eight-second rides, both with low scores. Pat was the one with a real knack for the sport—he won several events and went on to ride in his adult years. You can imagine my shock to learn that he was killed during a rodeo event in his adult years. It truly is a dangerous sport.

I had always been big for my age, but I had never been involved in team sports of any kind. I'd never shot hoops in my younger years, mostly because I didn't have any friends nearby to play with and basketball is a team sport. Even though I was inexperienced, I found that I wanted to learn how to play football. Seligman High School had a football team, and when I was in the seventh grade, I approached the coach and asked him if I could practice with the high school team. I wasn't trying to get on the team; I just wanted to learn to play the game. He agreed to let me join the practices, and I was quickly indoctrinated into the sport. The high school players were good about accepting me and teaching me the basics of football, but they showed no mercy at all when it came to tackling drills. I was lacking in experience, strength, stamina, and size, and it showed. During every practice, the field, consisting of dirt and gravel, became embedded in any skin that I'd left exposed. After every practice, I'd limp my way back to work at the White Horse Café and finish my shift, barely able to lift my arms.

Seligman did have a seventh grade basketball team, though, and the coach, noticing that I was already six feet tall, asked me to try out. Again, there was one problem—like I said earlier, I'd never played basketball. So the coach worked with me one-on-one when we had free time, teaching me the fundamentals, and I made the starting team. You could pick me out in a heartbeat. I really stuck out, being the only white, redheaded kid on the team—the rest being Native Americans who could run forever without getting winded. Overall, we were a good team, but we got many a chuckle when we visited other schools and our starting lineup was introduced. All of the Native American boys were announced first, followed by a tall, skinny, freckle-faced redhead named Frank Shankwitz playing center.

These opportunities were only made possible because other people gave me a chance—they were kind enough to take the time to teach a young, inexperienced boy how to play football and basketball. They took the time to practice and train with me, asking nothing in return for the favor. The same was true of so many other people who shared a meal with me and let me become a part of their family. While I didn't truly grasp the extent of their unselfish generosity at a young age, I came to understand that such acts weren't an exception—helping others was a way of life for them. It was Juan who reminded me to be grateful for the kindnesses and opportunities extended to me while growing up, and he didn't beat around the bush. Subtlety wasn't his style.

One day, he saw me and asked if I would be in the Snow Cap after school the next day.

"I can't. I have football practice," I explained.

"That's right. I forgot," he said. "How'd a kid like you get on the high school team?"

"I'm not really on the team. They just let me practice with them."

"That's an awfully nice coach, letting a junior high kid practice with his team." Then he placed a hand on my shoulder, and all joking aside, was serious as his eyes bore into mine. "You should be grateful for that, Frank. You should always be grateful for what people give to you."

Football - Prescott High

He let that sink in for a moment, then nodded and tousled my hair playfully. "Now get home before your mother starts to worry."

"I'm actually going to the Ortegas' house before I go home," I said. "I'm meeting Mom there."

"They feeding you supper again?"

"Yep, another bean and tortilla night." I smiled.

"That sure is nice of them. Make sure you thank them."

Juan never let me forget that people who didn't have much of their own always found a way to help me and my mother. He reminded me that I should always be grateful for their kindness and generosity and that it was something I should never take for granted or forget.

"Someday when you have something to give to somebody, make sure you do," he said.

* * *

I was in the sixth grade and had mentioned to Juan several times that I missed my father and knew he lived in Chicago but didn't know how to reach him. I didn't have his address or phone number, but I really wanted to let him know I was living in Arizona. Seligman still had the hand-crank telephone system, but mostly just for businesses. At that time, very few homes actually had a telephone. To use the hand-crank system, you'd pick up a phone, which was located in a separate building, and a central operator would answer and then transfer your call to the party you were calling.

One day, Juan took me to the telephone building and told the operator I would like to contact my father. She wrote down my dad's name and went to work in an attempt to connect us. After a great deal of plugging in cords and pulling others back out, she finally smiled and told us she was talking to an operator in Chicago. As it does to a kid on Christmas morning, the wait seemed like hours, then she suddenly jotted the information I needed on a piece of paper and handed it to me. There it was: Frank P. Shankwitz, Mulberry 5-4968, my father's phone number. Juan's big old grin went from ear to ear as he thanked the operator and we left. Number in hand, I didn't know what to do, but Juan explained it to me. We would wait until Saturday, when my father probably wasn't working, then Juan would show me how to make a long distance collect call to my father.

I didn't tell my mother I had my father's phone number. I just held onto it tightly and waited for what seemed like an eternity. When Saturday finally came, Juan took me to a phone at the town's general store. He proceeded to instruct me how to tell the operator, the same person who had found the phone number, that I wanted to place a long distance collect to my father's number from me, Frank Shankwitz, Jr. The phone rang several times before a man answered. As I started to say hello, the operator interrupted, saying she had a long distance collect call from Frank Shankwitz, Jr. and asked if he would accept the charges. There was a long pause and then my dad said, "Frankie—Frankie, yes, I'll accept the charges." I don't know who was more excited, me or my dad, as we started talking. Every three minutes the operator interrupted our conversation, saying, "Your three minutes are up; will you accept additional charges?" I have no idea how much that phone call cost my father but he kept accepting the additional charges. It seemed like we talked forever. I told him where I lived, our Post Office box number, and all about school and work. We ended the call by making arrangements for me to call him collect every Saturday morning, which I faithfully did. The owners at the White Horse Café had no problem with me leaving my job for a few minutes every Saturday to call my father, and I was grateful for that.

My mother was furious when I finally told her I had talked to my father and he knew where we lived. However, there was a silver lining—it was those phone calls that finally led my mother to talk to my father, which led to something even better. I finally was going to see my dad.

At the end of my seventh grade school year, my mother surprised me, saying she'd been in contact with my father and they'd worked out a deal for me to spend the summer with him in Chicago. Naturally, I was excited—I hadn't seen my father in several years and really missed him. However, I was reluctant to leave my job for fear I'd lose it. My mother explained that she'd already talked to the owners of the White Horse Café, who promised I'd still have a job when I returned. She even bought me a new shirt and pair of Levis for the trip, which I'd take on the train. Countless times I'd hauled ice to the engine of the El Capitan streamliner during its route from Los Angeles to Chicago, but now I was going to be a passenger on it as it headed east across the country. Knowing my job was safe until I returned, I was excited and ready to go, proudly wearing my new clothes. Everything was great, except my boots were too small and falling apart. There wasn't enough money to buy me new cowboy boots, so I rigged mine with a trick I'd learned from the Native American boys—I cut the toe off my boots and made another cut in the instep, then I wrapped the two back together, extending them with white athletic tape. It wasn't pretty, but it worked. With these "alterations," the boots fit my feet, but I have to admit I got some very strange looks from other passengers on the train.

The train ride was an adventure in itself. As I got settled in my seat on the El Capitan, the conductor appeared and told me to leave my bag overhead and come with him. He led me to the engine of the El Capitan, and I immediately recognized the engineer from the many times I'd hauled ice for him. He asked me if I would like to help him drive the Streamliner to Winslow, where they would change crews, and then I could go back to my regular seat. Boy, did I!

What a thrill! To this day, I can still remember going up, into, and over the snow-capped mountains, feeling like a king as I sat in the engineer seat, blowing the train whistle at the crossings. I was having a blast waving at the cars as the train ran parallel to Route 66, the same road that had taken us to Arizona. It was like a dream come true, and for a boy who didn't have much, I felt like the luckiest kid in the world.

It was a great summer. I loved every minute I spent with my dad, and I even got to meet my mom's father, Ben. Mom had never let me spend any time with him, but I liked him right away. He was tall, with thick, wavy hair and a big, friendly smile. We spent several days together that summer getting to know each other. I also spent time with my other grandparents, who I hadn't seen since I was a small child, as well as my mom's brother, Earle.

It was an easy, pleasant summer. Dad had a nice place to live and there was always food on the table. Every other Friday was payday, which meant it was pizza night—a novelty for me because I'd never tasted pizza before. One bite and I was hooked. They ordered a medium pizza just for me, and I ate the whole thing by myself, every other week. It was a new and rare treat, and like most kids my age, I looked forward to it.

In Chicago, I enjoyed being part of a real family with my dad, stepmother, and stepbrother. That was the one thing that was missing in my life out west—and it was as close as I'd ever gotten to being a part of a real traditional family. Yet, at the end of the summer when my dad asked me to stay and live with them, I realized I didn't want to. But it wasn't because I didn't love my dad. I did. City life just wasn't for me. I'd known that since the time I lived in Michigan. I'd become a cowboy at heart, and it's not an exaggeration to say that there aren't too many cowboys in Chicago, especially boys my age. If I stayed, I knew I'd always have nice clothes and an equally nice place to live, and I'd be surrounded by my family there, but I'd miss the horses, trains, and rodeos out west. I'd miss Juan and my friends. My father didn't argue, accepting it quite well when I told him I wanted to go back to Arizona, and he sent me off with some new jeans, new shirts, and a very committed and heartfelt promise never to lose contact with me again. Oh, and he also got me a brand new pair of cowboy boots.

The engineer knew when I was coming home from Chicago, and when the train stopped in Winslow en route to Seligman, I again was escorted to the engine and asked to help drive the El Capitan. It was the perfect cap to a fantastic summer. When the train arrived in Seligman, I saw my mother waiting for me and had fun blowing the train whistle and waving to her from the engine. She burst out laughing, and so did I.

But the laughter was short lived. When I returned to Seligman, I immediately began to regret my decision not to live with my father. Right away, I noticed that tires were being installed on our trailer. When I asked my mom why, she explained that she had a new job in Prescott, Arizona, and was moving the trailer with her. However, she also told me that she couldn't afford to move me there with her. Sensing what was coming, my heart fell. Since I had a good job in Seligman, she explained that I would stay there and finish eighth grade while she got settled. She had even arranged for me to move in with a Mexican lady who was a widow.

Not only was my mom moving away, leaving me behind, but I would be left to fend for myself. Just entering the eighth grade, I had to support myself without any assistance from my mother. Rent would cost me fifteen dollars a week. It included dinner every night, but I also had to do chores and help fix up the house. I only took home sixteen to twenty dollars a week from the White Horse Café, and that money went to my mother. That left me with the money I made hauling ice and working at the Snow Cap. Realizing this, I realized that maybe I should have stayed with my dad.

Most of all, though, I was angry—angry at my mother for leaving me to totally support myself. The anger I'd carried for some time because she'd prevented me from seeing my father for so many years resurfaced and intensified as I realized that my mom could so easily leave me behind. The many times she'd moved me from one place to another, state to state, in an attempt to put miles and time between my dad and me replayed in my head. I was confused and mad that she had done so given the fact that she was now leaving me, seemingly without a care or regret.

I didn't have much time to think about it, though, because Mom moved the next week, taking my home with her. As planned, I moved in with Ester, a woman I'd met before but didn't know very well. In her early fifties, Ester was a small but stout woman with graying black hair. Very stern, she lived by the book—always wearing a dress and just as rigid and inflexible regarding the house rules and chores. For all her sternness, though, she was generous with her appreciation and praise when chores were completed.

On the outside, her house was small and shabby, but I was used to that. However, on the inside, it was rather nice. I was pleasantly surprised, and excited, when she showed me my bedroom—a real bedroom, with a double bed, a dresser, and a nightstand. No more sleeping on the couch! Ester also had an indoor bathroom where I could take a shower. No more walking to the Santa Fe locker room to get clean! All in all, it was a step up for me, and I realized it wasn't so bad, after all.

As promised, Ester made my dinners. It was nice not to have to work for my evening meal or count on the kindnesses of others to set another place at their table to accommodate a hungry boy. I found that Ester was an excellent cook and she gave me generous portions of every Mexican dish I could imagine. I had breakfasts while working at the White Horse Café, and Chuy or his sister would bring me a burrito for lunch at school. After school and when I wasn't working, I pulled weeds from Ester's yard. Later, we repaired the front porch and put a coat of fresh paint on the outside. By the time we were done, the outside of the house wasn't too shabby anymore at all.

Living with Ester brought other "firsts" into my life. When Mom and I first arrived in Seligman, we had no television and the only phones were the old hand-cranked ones. Over time, though, the phone company had built a relay tower and power building, bringing newer technology and dial phones to the area. The man who worked there hooked a TV antenna up to the tower and, voilà, they had TV reception. Sometimes he'd load a group of us town kids into the back of his pickup truck and take us there to watch a show. It was a really big treat.

When we first arrived in Seligman, there was a movie theater in town. I remember that it was big enough to have a balcony and it cost twenty-five cents for a child's admission. Shortly after moving to Seligman, the movie house burned down and was not rebuilt. The priest at the Catholic church obtained a used 16mm movie projector and, somehow, had old cartoon movies shipped in every week. He would put up a sheet inside the church and, once a week, he invited all of the kids and parents to visit the church and watch the movies. It was usually a long evening due to the fact that he had to keep changing reels and repair the film with scotch tape every time the tape broke, which was often.

The town of Ash Fork was twenty-one miles east of Seligman, and when the freight trains passed through, they would either stop or slow down. Ash Fork also had a regular movie theater called The Yavapai Theater, which showed all the new "B" western movies. The train crews in Seligman would let some of us kids get on a empty freight train flatcar, never inside an empty boxcar because the door could slide shut and we'd be trapped inside, and ride to Ash Fork. Once there, the engineer would either stop or slow down enough for us to jump off. After the movie, we would stand by the tracks waiting for a westbound train. When an engineer who knew us saw us, he would either stop or slow down enough for us to jump on a flatcar. The trains always stopped in Seligman, so it was no problem for us getting off.

Before long, though, television became more common, and we frequently learned that more and more people had TVs in their own homes and were able to receive a couple stations.

One night after returning to Ester's after work, she met me in the living room. A broad smile spread across her face as she looked at something that was covered with a sheet. She carefully pulled the sheet off to unveil another wonderful surprise—a brand new television that had an outside antenna that could pick up two stations! From that moment, my mind shifted from thinking that my mother had left, moving away and leaving me to take care of and support myself, to realizing that, for the first time, I had my own bed and bedroom, a fantastic hot dinner every single night, a real shower, and now television. Suddenly, I realized that I was doing better on my own than I ever had done when living with her. I began to think that I could take care of myself, after all.

Chapter Five
Another Day, Another Opportunity

As the months passed by, I was surprised how well I adapted to my mother's absence. Given our lifestyle and financial difficulties throughout the years, I'd learned how to take care of myself, mostly out of necessity. I continued working, making sure I could afford to pay for my rent and other necessities. However, in Seligman, I didn't stand out from the other kids. In this blue-collar town, I wasn't the poorest kid around. In fact, I fit in rather well with my classmates and friends. They, too, worked to help support their families, most of which were low income and counted on additional income from their kids' jobs to scrape by from one payday to the next.

While work consumed the majority of my after-school time, my last year in junior high wasn't all work, and thanks to Juan, I became involved in extracurricular activities. In many ways, Juan acted as both a boss and a friend, and sometimes as a substitute parent, as he encouraged and supported me in pursuing outside activities. In the eighth grade, I continued to practice football with the high school team and kept playing basketball, too. It was Juan who also encouraged me to play drums in the high school band.

I never thought of myself as being musically talented and probably wouldn't have pursued learning how to play an instrument on my own. When I was in the fifth grade, though, one of the kids in the high school band gave me a pair of old drumsticks, although I didn't have any formal lessons in using them or actual drums that I could beat them on. But I was innovative and figured out a way to play along to the radio. The only radio station we could receive during the day in Seligman was Navajo, but in the evening, we were able to pick up the infamous Wolfman Jack show out of Oklahoma City. While listening to Wolfman Jack on the radio at night, I'd beat my drumsticks on the bottom of a garbage can and pretend I was actually playing the drums. That's as far as my interest went—until seventh grade, when a new music teacher arrived at our school. Decidedly different than any of our other teachers, he wore suits and ties every day. Even more impressive, we learned that he was from Los Angeles and had played trumpet in the Harry James Band. To us, he was big time, the real thing, which sparked a newfound interest in music for the entire school. Many of the Mexican and Native American students already had a natural musical talent, which he was able to further develop. With his instruction and inspiration, by the end of the year, our school's marching band was even winning state honors. With that success driving him, he decided to also develop a school dance band.

Given the fact that I had never taken any professional lessons or had any other form of instruction, I was surprised when the music teacher approached me and offered to teach me how to really play the drums and read music. I gladly accepted, and by the time I was in the eighth grade, I was a real member of the band, playing drums in both the marching band and the school dance band.

Then our teacher started his own dance band—one that was separate from the school. I was shocked—and admittedly pleased—when he asked me to play drums in his band, but I had to turn him down because I didn't have my own set of drums and wouldn't be allowed to use the school's drums outside of school. Reluctantly, he accepted my reasons when I declined his offer, knowing it was an obstacle I couldn't overcome. A few weeks later, though, he asked me to meet him in the music room. When I arrived, I couldn't believe my eyes. Right there in front of me was a complete drum set, with my initials painted on the bass drum. It was more than a surprise. Elated, I asked him where they came from: how had he been able to do this? He explained that he'd driven to Prescott, where he found the drum set at a pawn shop for forty dollars. He told me that not only were the drums really mine, but I'd also be allowed to keep them at school in the music room. With that, I became the newest member of his dance band.

Much like our basketball team, our band was an interesting sight to behold—a spectacle to the eyes that certainly attracted attention and interest. Our dance band consisted of four members: our music teacher playing his shiny trumpet while decked out in a nice suit and tie, a Mexican on bass fiddle, an Native American on the piano, and me, a redheaded, freckle-faced eighth grader called Pancho on the drums. We were as diverse as we could possibly be in that town, or in the local bars where we played in towns surrounding Seligman. Each gig paid me ten dollars, and it wasn't long until I'd earned enough to pay my music teacher back the forty dollars for my drums.

Me on the drums

Between working at the White Horse Café and the Snow Cap, hauling ice at the Santa Fe Railroad, doing chores for Ester, playing basketball and football, and being a member of the school and dance bands, eighth grade passed rather quickly. Before I knew it, it was time for graduation.

A couple days before the big event, there was a knock at Ester's door. When I opened it, I was speechless and couldn't believe my eyes . . . Before me stood my dad, *my dad!* He'd driven all the way from Chicago to Arizona to watch me graduate and was staying at the Supai Motel, where my mother used to work. The Supai Motel was a typical roadside motel—a one-story motel, with rooms side by side, all accessible by exterior doors. Because it was on

Route 66, it was a popular motel that had frequent guests and had always been maintained well. Still, it wasn't Chicago, better known for its upscale and fancier accommodations, and I worried that my dad might find it to be subpar. But when we went back to the motel to catch up and talk, he seemed to be quite content and at home. If he felt even a hint of dissatisfaction with his surroundings, he didn't show it in any way.

When we arrived at the motel, my father gave me my second surprise—a brand new suit that he'd bought for me to wear at my graduation. Dad always knew that my wardrobe was sparse and worn, and whenever he got the chance to see me, he made an effort to make sure I left with new clothes that fit. That wasn't the only surprise he had in store, though. Later, he took me to the White Horse Café for dinner. This time, I was a guest and didn't have to bus tables or wash dishes. It was a real treat, especially since I was sharing it with my dad.

There were about ten students in my graduating class—most of their families didn't have two dimes to rub together, and it showed in the way they dressed. There I was in my brand new suit, along with my father, Frank Sr., who was wearing a nice suit and tie accompanied by shiny wingtip shoes. He looked like the stereotypical businessman from the big city, and although it should not have embarrassed me at all, I'm a little ashamed to say it did. For the first time, I saw Seligman and its people through my father's eyes, and vice versa. I was afraid my father would turn away from these people who had taken me in, given me jobs, and been so generous to me, judging them based on their worn cowboy boots and plain workingman blue jeans. I was also a little concerned that the people of Seligman would do the same and shy away from my dad out of jealousy, thinking he was above them, or at least believe he thought he was.

Almost immediately, my father put my worries to rest. One of his first requests was that I introduce him to all of the people in town who had helped me in any way so he could personally thank them. His appreciation was genuine and sincere.

"I've heard so much about you," he said with an arm outstretched to Juan.

With his natural good nature, Juan replied, "Well, I hope it was all good stuff."

As the two shared a laugh, I was relieved. Both men were at ease, and there was no evidence of judgment on either side.

"It sure was, and I appreciate all you've done for my son."

"He's a good kid," Juan said, looking at my father. "I know he'll do well."

This comfortable camaraderie continued as I introduced Dad to other people in Seligman. He seemed to take a genuine interest in knowing who they were and learning about the people who had molded my life for the last several years. Still, at the end of the night, I was slightly surprised when I watched my father extend his arms, giving Juan a hug before he departed.

"So long," he said.

"We'll see ya," Juan replied. It was good-bye and time to go. My father and I turned to leave Juan and Seligman, on our way to Prescott, Arizona, where I would be living with my mother once again.

* * *

A beautiful, quaint town on a high desert mountain, Prescott is about eighty miles from Seligman. I loved the town but missed my friends in Seligman and, of course, Juan. But I had no choice—it was time for me to move in with my mom. My mother had actually found a trailer park for her trailer, so this time we had full access to heat, electricity, and hot water. It was definitely a step-up from the last time I lived in the trailer, which became my home for the next four years while I attended high school.

Again, one of my first orders of business was to find a job, and it didn't take long. My first job was unloading furniture for a secondhand store, a physical job that helped boost my muscle mass and built me up for football. For the first time, I was old enough to try out for a team, and I found the years of practice with Seligman's high school team gave me an advantage that earned me a spot on the football team right away. School, however, posed a challenge—it seemed that Seligman's academic standards were behind those deemed acceptable by Prescott's school district, and testing showed that I was significantly behind in math. The solution posed was to hold me back and have me return to the eighth grade. Again, folks stepped up to help me. My football coaches offered to privately tutor me after school to bring me up to speed. After a few weeks, I passed the math test and was, therefore, able to stay in high school and on the football team.

My next job was at Safeway, where I worked throughout high school, starting out as a bag boy and doing carry-out. Eventually, I was promoted to stocker and clerk. The job was a good one, and the manager worked my schedule around football practice and games. With a flexible schedule, I was always scheduled off on away games, and when we had a home game, I was allowed to attend the after-game dance, then go in at 10 p.m. to stock shelves. My coaches, employers, and teachers all commended the work ethic I'd learned in Seligman and also encouraged me to do well in my studies and at work.

During this time, I was living with my mother, but any closeness we had ever had, if there had been any mother-son bonding, had distanced itself throughout the years. I had never truly forgiven my mother for keeping my father out of my life throughout most of my childhood. She had spent most of her life rebelling against city life and the traditional roles of wife and mother. If she had any maternal instincts, she rarely shared or showed them. I was old enough now to understand and accept that. Out of necessity, I had learned to take care of myself, but outside of my father, the people who raised and molded me the most were Juan and the good people of Seligman and Prescott who went out of their way to take the time to make a positive impact on the life of a fair-skinned, redheaded boy called Pancho. Out of the goodness of their hearts, they took me under their wings and, as a result, became lifelong friends whom I will treasure for the rest of my life.

Chapter Six
Tomorrow Is Here

Life after high school poses a dilemma for many. What do I want to be when I grow up? Can I, will I, should I go to college? When I graduated from high school, college wasn't the traditional and obvious next step—many graduates chose to go into the trades or pursue other paths where additional education wasn't required. Some went to work full-time at the family ranch or business, while yet others continued working at their part-time jobs, working their way up the ladder.

I had decided early on that I couldn't afford to go to college, and although I had been offered a management training position at Safeway, I turned it down. During high school, I became interested in air traffic control, so I researched the Air Force and liked what I learned. I took the Air Force entrance exam, qualified for air traffic control school, and joined the Air Force in November 1961. A friend drove me to Phoenix from Prescott, and I was sworn in in Phoenix and then flown to San Antonio, Texas, to start basic training at Lackland Air Force Base. I was an official member of the United States military.

My work ethic and participation in high school sports had prepared me well for basic training. For me, it was a snap. I was usually in the top three in completing the obstacle course. One of my training instructors was really into physical fitness, and after spending the day training, he'd invite me to run the obstacle course with him, the reward at the end being a couple cans of cold beer. Another training instructor who had been on President Truman's Honor Guard took notice of my marching and began giving me private lessons in marching and commands, which paid off years later when I was stationed in England.

During basic training, I was appointed a squad leader and later became the flight leader. When basic training came to an end, like the other members of my squad, I awaited the order for my school. Along with several others, I had requested air traffic control school, two were going to Russian language schools, and more preferred various tech schools. Much to our surprise, and disappointment, our entire class of fifty was assigned to the Air Police, to be sent to various Air Force bases throughout the United States, and I was assigned to Walker Air Force Base in Roswell, New Mexico. Our initial requests had been altered to "meet the needs of the Air Force." Not able to do anything about it, I accepted my assignment and vowed to make the best of it.

In high school, I truly enjoyed history and was especially interested in learning about World War II. So when it came time to request my assignments in the Air Force, I wanted to go overseas to England, Germany, and Spain. However, the Air Force assigns you where you are needed, and I was sent to a Strategic Air Command base in Roswell, New Mexico, to provide flight line security for B-52s and Atlas missiles, as well as security for the base perimeter. I found I enjoyed the assignment, working outdoors and the challenge of New Mexico winters. However, I had another challenge—my income from the Air Force was significantly less than I'd been making at Safeway, and I needed to find a way to make some extra money. For one thing, the Air Police were required to have tailored fatigue and dress uniforms, unlike the other airmen. Not only were they required to be tailored, but they also had to be starched and pressed. Tailoring was more expensive than most airmen could afford on their pay, and the laundry on the base charged extra to starch uniforms. To answer these two needs—uniforms that met our requirements and the need for additional income—my roommate and I came up with a plan. He had worked in a tailor shop when he was a civilian, and I had been ironing my own clothes for years. We each made an investment—he purchased a sewing machine, and I bought an iron, ironing board, and cans of spray starch, and we were in business. We spent nearly all of our off time tailoring and pressing uniforms and shining boots, and made enough money doing it that we were able to take a trip into town every other week and enjoy ourselves.

However, I was only at the New Mexico base for a few months before I was reassigned—this time, to the Minuteman Missile security duty at Malstrom Air Force Base in Great Falls, Montana. I'd never been to Montana before, but I liked it immediately because it reminded me of the mountains in northern Arizona, but more extreme. I set up shop right away and continued my ironing business, and before long, I was making enough extra cash to explore the area and even enjoy some of Montana's wonderful fishing spots. I warmed to the state and began making plans to live there after I completed my years with the Air Force.

My security duties enabled me to see some amazing country. The Air Police drove with the missile crew to a remote missile control center, located well over a hundred miles from the base. The actual missile site was usually another hundred miles from the control center. When a sensor at the missile site alerted the crew that an intruder had breached the site, the Air Police would be alerted and scramble via helicopter to search and secure the site. Most of the time, these intrusions were false alarms caused by animals. When that happened, the sensors would be reset and we were allowed to go back to the missile center, via helicopter, the long way—where we got to enjoy a spectacular view of Yellowstone National Park or Glacier National Park. In the event, though, that the sensors couldn't be reset, for whatever reason, we would have to stay on site until they were operational, sometimes for a day or longer. Because there were no indoor facilities on the site, we carried a go-bag containing clothing for cold weather (the temperature at night in Montana fell below zero) and extra C-rations. On more than one occasion, we stayed on site for up to three days. When that happened, a helicopter would drop off additional water and rations to get us through.

It was a plan that worked well—everyone was prepared to do what had to be done and carried out their duties as efficiently and quickly as possible. However, one unexpected event can implode even the most refined and efficient military operations. Ours was a snowstorm—not just any snowstorm, but a fast and fierce storm that left us stranded, without shelter, and without aid.

The storm had just begun when we arrived at the missile center, and temperatures were predicted to fall well below zero. The wheels were set in motion when one of the missile site intrusion alarms was activated, and the helicopter crew rushed me and my partner to one of the more remote sites. As luck would have it, the sensors couldn't be reset, requiring us to remain on the site. The helicopter crew left us there only to quickly find that the storm had grown in intensity to the point that they could not make it back to the missile center, so they were diverted to a small airport in a nearby town.

Our one day's worth of C-rations and cold weather

clothing were no match for the impending storm, even if we were left there for only one night. We might have been without adequate food and shelter, but we did have support. The missile site had telephone communication, and the missile crew called us every hour to check on our welfare. Knowing we weren't going anywhere in the near future, my partner and I became aware that if we were to survive the brutal wind chills and blowing and drifting snow, we'd have to create a makeshift snow fort to protect ourselves from the elements as much as possible. As night loomed, the snow and drifts had risen to well over four feet and the temperature had plummeted. We had no fuel to make a fire and no other source of heat or protection. The missile center called us and advised that a rescue operation was underway trying to get to our location, but it would take time. The storm had grounded the helicopters and the four-wheel drive vehicles couldn't get through. That left us with one hope—the snow cat vehicles, which we were informed were trying to get to us. Help was on the way, but nobody knew when they would arrive. For the first time, I realized just how defenseless we really were.

While I never fought in a war and came face-to-face with enemy gunfire or experienced a do-or-die situation where my life was in immediate peril, I had been prepared for such situations. Air Force training emphasized survivor skills. We were expected to do our job . . . and to do everything in our power to stay alive. We'd been taught how to survive in extreme situations and knew that being able to assess a situation and make decisions with a level head could mean the difference between life and death. This wasn't war, but we were under enemy attack. That enemy was Mother Nature, and she had hurled her fury with a vengeance, leaving us weaponless and open to attack from all sides. We'd been sent here to do a job—now, we had to put our training to use—our mission was to stay alive.

The rescue operation took three days. Long before, we'd run out of rations, as well as water. We were both suffering from dehydration, hypothermia, frostbite, and extreme hunger and were in need of emergency medical care when they arrived. Air medics had accompanied the snow cat crew to provide us with immediate first aid before beginning the slow trip back to a main highway, where an Air Force ambulance was standing by, waiting to escort us to the base hospital. I don't recall much of the trip and wasn't aware of much that was going on, with the exception of the fact that I couldn't seem to warm my fingers and my feet were burning with a searing pain, as though they were on fire. Once we were transferred to the ambulance and had begun the long trip to the base hospital, the weather cleared enough that a helicopter was able to pick us up and transport us much more quickly by air than the emergency vehicles could on treacherous icy, snow-covered roads.

We were treated at the base hospital. The first order of business was to get our core temperatures back to normal.

We had both lost a lot of weight as well. The doctors explained that this was not only due to the cold and lack of food, but also due to the calories burned from the extreme shivering our body had done in an attempt to keep itself warm. Never one to turn down a meal, I enjoyed the extra meals and milkshakes between meals they gave us to help us restore the weight we'd lost. With efforts being made to restore our body temperatures and weight, the medical staff addressed the other effects of our long-term exposure to the frigid elements. My worst ailment was frostbite on my toes and fingers, but I eventually recovered. My partner, on the other hand, had such severe frostbite that they were unable to reverse the damage. He had to have several fingers and toes amputated, thus putting an abrupt and unfortunate end to his Air Force career.

After nearly a week of treating my frostbite and hydrating and nourishing my body, I was well enough to get on my feet and begin physical therapy so I could walk again. It's easy to think that therapy would be a breeze, but I was wrong and had underestimated the effects of frostbite. The female medic assigned to me was relentless; the therapy itself was brutal. She wouldn't let me ease up, even a little, when the pain became too much to bear. I was more than grateful to have finished a particularly grueling therapy session and was finally resting back in my hospital bed when the staff was called to attention. The base commander had entered the ward, and as protocol warranted, everyone snapped to attention. After his presence was announced, to my surprise, he walked over to my bed. Once he'd made the dutiful inquiries about my welfare and progress, he apologized that the rescue effort had taken so long, explaining once again that the severe snowstorm had hindered the operation. He continued, telling me that he had reviewed my records and noticed that upon graduation from basic training, I had requested assignments in England, Germany, and Spain. Naturally, those requests had not been approved. Smiling, he proceeded to inform me that he had been authorized to transfer me to any base I desired, including Arizona or Montana if that's what I wanted, as a thank-you for my service and efforts. I couldn't believe what I was hearing, and it took a second for it to sink in . . . but it only took me a moment to respond. I wanted to be transferred to England. The commander told me to consider it done—as soon as I was released from the hospital and cleared for duty, I'd be on my way. It wasn't how I wanted to get that assignment, but I'd take it! Excited and motivated by my upcoming transfer, I decided to facilitate my release from the hospital and doubled my sessions with the therapy medic, despite the pain. My efforts paid off, and within a month, I was released on my way to England.

My fascination with England began in high school. An honor student in U.S. and world history, I was especially interested in the history of World War II in both Europe and the Pacific. The first Air Force base I was assigned to in England was RAF Greenham Common, a World War II British Air Base that had been converted to a joint U.S. Air Force Strategic Air Command B-47 and Royal Air Force Bomber Base. Rich with history, it was precisely what I wanted and exactly like I'd envisioned. The building and open bay barracks were built in World War II, with some small modern changes made over the years. To me, it was like living in my high school history books.

Shortly after my arrival, I reopened my ironing business. Soon I had made enough extra money to afford my first train trip into London on a three-day pass. For the next three years, I used all of my three-day passes to explore London and all of England, especially those areas involving the Battle of Britain. There was so much to learn and see, and I was fascinated. It had only been seventeen years since World War II had ended, and England hadn't been totally rebuilt. My sightseeing excursions took me to many bomb-damaged buildings and relics from the War. It was a once-in-a-lifetime education that I treasure to this day.

After a year at RAF Greenham Common, I was transferred to yet another joint Strategic Air Command—the Royal Air Force Bomber Base RAF Upper Heyford, which is where I spent the remainder of my Air Force career. B-47 bomber crews flew their bombers to our base from the States for thirty-day temporary assignments. During that time, they would get a five-day break. That break provided me with an opportunity to make some pocket money, so I hung up my iron and ironing board and started a tour guide business.

Through my sightseeing endeavors, I now knew London like the back of my hand and had visited both the tourist and World War II historic sites often. I knew I could capitalize on my experience, so I posted flyers in the officers' club advertising two-day escorted tours of London. Using my three-day pass, I was able to conduct two tours a month, with as many as twelve officers joining each tour. I charged ten dollars per person and made about $240 a month, which was twice as much as my Air Force pay. The tours gave me an opportunity to continue to see London and share my knowledge of the sites with the bomber crew officers, while making money. Being paid for what I wanted to do, what I loved to do, was a win-win, and I didn't take it for granted.

During my last year in the Air Force, our Strategic Air Command Base was transitioned into a joint U.S. Air Force/NATO Tactical Fighter Base. My Air Police duties switched from flight line/bomber security to Base Police duties, which included actual police work, including writing traffic violations, investigating traffic accidents, and conducting criminal investigations. These duties also included participating and marching in several formal ceremonies. My Air Police sergeant took note of my marching abilities and submitted my name to be a member of the base Honor Guard, and I was selected. This led to one of the more personal memorable experiences during my Air Force career.

In school, my interest in World War II history included the study of Sir Winston Churchill. I took that fascination with me to London, and it compelled me to include

Air Force Honor Guard - England

10 Downing Street in my guided tours, mainly because I could imagine Mr. Churchill in residence there during the war—again, I found it very intriguing to relive history. Unfortunately, on January 24, 1965, Sir Winston Churchill died. His funeral procession started at St. Paul's Cathedral in London and traveled to the tiny village of Bladon, with his final resting place located in the cemetery at St. Martin's Church. I was selected to be a part of the joint

military forces Honor Guard on the last leg of the funeral and burial procession. I was honored to pay tribute to this great man and provide him with the military procession he undoubtedly deserved. I found that duty rather easy to carry out, for I had a profound respect for him. The most difficult part of that detail, though, was trying to remain at attention, standing totally still, while a tear silently spilled from my eye and trickled down my cheek.

U.S. Air Force - 1965

Base Batrol - RAF Upper Heyford

The Air Force gave its members a thirty-day personal leave each year. The majority of the airmen stationed overseas would wait until they had accumulated the entire thirty days and use their leave to return to the States to visit their parents, girlfriends, and families. It gave them an opportunity to spend time with their loved ones, and I couldn't blame them for looking forward to their month-long return home. However, I decided to take advantage of my leave and use it as a way to travel Europe, visiting even more historic World War II battle and historic sites. Our base had weekly flights to Munich, Germany, which became my starting point. From there, I'd catch a bus or train, or even hitchhike, throughout Europe. It was a valuable education that I would have never been able to receive . . . if it had not been for that one fateful snowstorm in Montana.

My time in London wasn't all spent working and touring the sights, though; I managed to squeeze in time for a social life as well. During my frequent trips to London, I met Mary, a young lady from Ireland, and we began dating. Mary was a dancer at the London Palladium, a position that has the same prestige as being one of the Radio City Music Hall Rockettes. She was tall, almost six feet in heels, and all legs, like most professional dancers. I'd often watch her performances, and Mary and I were occasionally invited to after-show parties for some of the up-and-coming musical acts. When Mary got off work, the pubs and clubs in London were getting ready to close, as English laws put last call for liquor at 11:00 p.m. There were several private clubs that could serve members liquor until 1:00 a.m., though, and Mary, being in the entertainment business, knew several of the owners; so even though we weren't members, we were allowed to enter the clubs. I had explained to Mary that, because I was an enlisted man, I couldn't afford to buy many drinks. That wasn't a problem, she said, since most of the clubs had live bands for dancing and the patrons would buy our drinks just to watch us dance. Never being light on my feet, I told her that wouldn't work. She assured me I'd do just fine—just follow her to the dance floor and she would do the rest. That's exactly what I did. I was just kind of out there as Mary danced, always wowing the crowd. I was a terrible dancer, but Mary was obviously good enough for both of us since we never paid for a drink at those clubs.

These post-performance parties offered another perk. That's how I came to meet The Dave Clark Five, Jerry and the Pacemakers, Lulu, Dusty Springfield, Petula Clark, and the legendary Beatles—before they became household names and had earned their claim to fame. While I thoroughly enjoyed personally meeting these musicians, they also found something unique in me that interested them a great deal. They really got a kick out of being with a Yank from Arizona and would ask questions about cowboys and Indians, believing that Arizona was still the old Wild West, since it had only been a state since 1912. Looking back, it's kind of ironic that *they* were so interested in *me,* when in fact it should have been the other way around. At the time, though, little did I know that I was hanging out with some of our future's most famous musical groups. Truly, I was among stars being born.

One of the more famous nightclubs in London was the Talk of the Town. Mary informed me that we had been invited to join a group there for dinner and it would be a special evening. While stationed in Montana, I started reading Ian Fleming's James Bond books, enjoying the adventures of 007 so much that I read all the books I could find. In 1962, the first James Bond film was released, starring Sean Connery, and Mary and I saw the movie when it opened in London. We were enjoying dinner at the Talk of the Town when I noticed several people walking up to a gentleman sitting at a table, shaking his hand, and taking photos. After a while, Mary, with a big smile on her face, led me to that table and introduced me to the gentleman sitting there. I was starstruck as I stared into the face of James Bond, 007. Mr. Connery invited us to join him for a few minutes before he had to leave. I tried to tell him how much I enjoyed his movie, but he learned I was from Arizona and, as strange as it may sound, that is what he wanted to talk about. I was in heaven and couldn't believe how lucky I was to be having a face-to-face discussion with the famous Sean Connery. Before he left, I managed to get his autograph, which I still have today.

At our base exchange (BX) at Upper Heyford, I met another woman—a new female sales clerk at the BX who'd caught my eye. A cute blond named Sue, she was the daughter of a lieutenant colonel on the base, I learned, which meant she was off-limits to an enlisted man. However, after making small talk with her for a few months while at the BX, it appeared that we had a mutual interest in each other, so I asked her out for a date. She said yes, with one caveat—I would have to receive permission from her father. It was a reasonable request, and one I was obliged to honor. I was relieved when the Colonel did, in fact, grant me permission to date his daughter. From then on, there were no more tours of London and England with officers, but rather the tours were with my new girlfriend, who seemed to enjoy my knowledge of the country as we visited its historic sites.

Soon, Sue and I were dating steadily. We were, as they say, a couple. We made it official in August of 1965, when we were married at the base chapel at RAF Upper Heyford. I had planned a honeymoon in London, but her father, the colonel, surprised us with his gift of airline tickets and accommodations in Paris. It was a wonderful wedding gift and a better honeymoon than I would have been able to afford on my salary. Although it wasn't my first trip to Paris (I had made several trips to France and Paris throughout my years in England), having a new bride in tow to share the sights of the charming city certainly made that trip much more fun and memorable.

Three months later, I made another trip—I was being discharged. I was going home.

Chapter Seven
Sweet Home Arizona

In November 1965, my enlistment with the Air Force was completed, and I was transferred to McGuire Air Force Base in New Jersey for an honorable discharge. Because I was an enlisted man, the Air Force would not authorize transportation for my spouse, so Sue remained in England with her parents until I could make arrangements for her to join me and we could begin to build our life together in the States.

While stationed in New Jersey, I contacted a former roommate I had while living in England. Richard lived in the Atlantic City area, where his family owned a fish delivery service. He offered to let me stay with him and deliver fish for their company when I was discharged so I could earn the money I needed for airfare to get my wife from England to the States. I also had to manage transportation of our car—a small English sports car we'd purchased in England.

I stayed in New Jersey and worked, religiously saving

money until the day I could send for my wife. Luckily, Sue and our car arrived in the States at about the same time. We stayed with Richard for a short time and then started the journey to our new home. As we traveled the highways, moving from the east coast across the Midwest and Great Plains, we never had to search for a motel room. All I had to do was contact one of the many people I'd met in the Air Force, and, without hesitation, they opened their homes to us for the night. These visits made the long journey west more enjoyable and gave me something to look forward to from day to day as we crossed from one state into another.

Our destination was Arizona. While I might have become more traveled and been exposed to other cities, states, and countries during my years in the Air Force, Arizona was still home. I'd never lost my love for the people, the land, and the way of life. It had ingrained itself into my blood, so much so that when it came time to make a home with my new wife, there was no question where we'd stake our roots.

However, there were other plans and decisions that had to be made, and I started making some of them while I was still in the Air Force. Being a newlywed, it was important to me to know that I had a job lined up when I got out of the service. So, while I was still in England, I contacted my former boss at the Safeway store in Prescott to see if he had any openings available. Not only did he say I could have my old job, but he also told me he'd put me in management training. It was a good offer that held some promise for a higher income and advancement. Shortly after, though, my mom, who was now working in Phoenix for Motorola, advised me that Motorola was offering preferential hiring of Vietnam-era veterans, and the starting pay was significantly more than I would make at Safeway. Knowing that, I decided not to return to Prescott, instead opting to go straight to Phoenix, where I would apply for a job at Motorola.

While I'd been overseas, my mother had made some life changes. She got a new job and had moved the old travel trailer to a run-down trailer park in Phoenix. She also remarried and moved to a small rental house with her new husband. That meant my wife and I had a place to live—not with my mom, but in the old travel trailer I'd lived in while growing up. In my mind, it would make a great starter home until I had steady work and had saved enough money to find nicer housing. So while I was still in England, I made the necessary arrangements, putting utilities in my name. To me, it was the perfect setup.

It never occurred to me, though, that my wife would disagree. You can imagine the look on my wife's face when we arrived in Phoenix and I pulled the car up to the trailer—her new home. I guess I'd gotten so used to the trailer that I never imagined how it would look to someone seeing it for the first time. It didn't help that she was an officer's daughter and had enjoyed a more privileged life. Having come from the grandeur of officer's base housing, she stared in shock at what was now "home sweet home"—an old, beat-up, outdated trailer in a run-down, low-income trailer park.

It certainly wasn't the life I wanted to provide for my wife, and unlike my mom, it was my intention that our housing situation would be temporary—we could get by with it until we could afford something better. It was quickly obvious, though, that we needed to speed up the process. Finding different housing was a priority—anything would be a step up. Thankfully, that happened sooner than I thought it would. I got a job at Motorola, and so did my wife. We were making a decent living, and within six months, we were able to get a VA loan and purchase a small, but nice, older home in a good part of town. Things were looking up.

Promotions came quick at Motorola, and it wasn't long before my wife and I were both promoted. Now that I was in a supervisor position, Motorola started sending me to engineering classes, and I also started college utilizing the GI Bill, taking advantage of some of my military benefits. We were doing quite well financially, and within three years, we were able to purchase our second home—a beautiful, brand-new home. It was a far cry from the old travel trailer, and we were content.

Motorola encouraged me to take several math courses in college, with a concentration in statistical analysis. For some reason that I really cannot justify, it clicked, and I did quite well. I was promoted again, this time to a technical engineering position responsible for analyzing components for possible failure rate. At this stage, my life revolved around work and furthering my education. I worked a lot of overtime at Motorola, and when it was quitting time, I'd go straight to my night classes at the college instead of going home. I also worked weekends. Yes, I had a great work ethic and wanted to better myself to become a better employee and provider, but it came at a price—I was never home.

Because I was gone so often and my wife was alone so much, she started using her vacation time to visit her parents, who had transferred to Ohio from England. At the time, I resented those visits and being left alone, not realizing that it was my own doing—after all, my wife was alone most of the time. Naturally, spending most of our time apart did not bode well for our marriage. We both wanted it to work, and we both wanted to have children. Hoping that a baby would strengthen our marriage and create a family unit, we welcomed our first daughter, Christine, in 1969. Our second daughter, Denise, was born in 1971, making us a family of four. My wife was no longer alone. But that didn't mean I was home more often—Motorola promoted me one more time, and I again made the mistake of working a lot of overtime, and not surprisingly, our marriage further deteriorated.

We loved our daughters, our home, and enjoyed a stable and secure income, but I still spent the majority of my time at work. It was a good job, with excellent pay and good coworkers and supervisors. Yet it wasn't my dream job. I found I was bored doing the same thing day after day. In addition, Motorola had begun laying off employees. They assured me that my job was not in jeopardy, but I knew there was no guarantee and felt apprehensive with every new quarter. To top it off, I was growing weary of living in Phoenix. The city life that I'd walked away from in my youth didn't suit me at all, and whenever we could, my wife and I would visit Prescott when I had a free day. I longed to return there and enjoy the western life I'd grown to love as a child.

Several of my high school classmates had joined the Arizona Highway Patrol and kept encouraging me to apply. They advised that being a veteran and having a college background could possibly allow me to place high in the testing process. Still, I had been at Motorola for seven years and was making good money—I had a wife, two daughters, and a nice new home. Risking the security of our income, home, and family wasn't in the cards, at least not initially. But I was interested. The thought of raising our daughters in a smaller town, where people knew each other and they could enjoy the way of life I grew up in, was appealing. I also knew that being a police officer would be far from boring, and I'd be doing more than analyzing numbers all day long. On a whim, I decided to apply and see what happened.

A month later, I was invited to start the testing process for the Arizona Highway Patrol. Placing high on the written test, I also passed the physical test and background check and placed high on the oral board. Several weeks later, while still working at Motorola, I received a letter from the highway patrol stating that I'd passed all tests. Out of one thousand applicants, I was one of fifty that were being hired. At the age of twenty-nine, I quit my job and entered the Patrol Academy in August of 1972.

While I was older than the majority of my classmates, the discipline I'd received in the Air Force and study habits I'd developed while taking college classes for Motorola helped me a great deal. The extensive courses I'd taken in math came in very handy, especially since we weren't allowed to use slide rules at the academy. Before I knew it, I'd graduated from the academy and was a sworn highway patrol officer assigned to Yuma, Arizona, which was more than 150 miles from our home in Phoenix.

Again, our family had to move. I'd taken a drastic cut in pay when I joined the highway patrol, far less than I had been making as an assistant engineer. But we made it work—we sold our home in Phoenix, netting a nice profit that not only allowed us to purchase a nice home in Yuma, but also left us with a big enough nest egg that my wife could be a stay-at-home mom and raise our children on a full-time basis. In the end, it had turned out to be a good career move—for me, for my wife, and our girls.

Every arrest during the wild Easter detail days on the

Colorado River has a story related to it, most routine, with a few that stand out because of the resulting humor. Bill Hansen and I had completed booking a couple of prisoners at the Parker jail and headed back up river to complete our shift. It had been one of those 110-degree days when we started our bookings in the late afternoon. Now it was mid-evening, and the temperature had cooled to a comfortable eighty degrees, with a nice breeze blowing off the river. The moon was full, bright enough to light up and making it easy to identify the surrounding area. Traffic was light and it was one of those times when your "patrolling" was more like just cruising.

The moment was broken by an oncoming single headlight weaving from one side of the highway to the other, no doubt another impaired driver. We both activated the emergency lights on our motorcycles and noted that the approaching vehicle was an off-road-type motorcycle, not legal for highway use. The approaching motorcycle rider played "chicken" with us, coming into our lane and driving straight at our lights. We noted he was driving slowly, and we simply split as he came at us, the driver laughing and waving as he passed us. The driver was twice the size of the off-road motorcycle he was riding, wearing only a pair of cut-offs and sunglasses. Though we turned and pulled up next to the driver and yelled for him to pull over, the driver just laughed and tried to ram my motorcycle, all at about ten miles per hour. Bill was laughing as the driver again tried to ram me, and said, "Take him out." To take him out meant to kick the rear of the driver's motorcycle, which usually causes the driver to lose control and crash. With no traffic in the area and going at such a slow speed, I did just that, which caused the motorcycle to swerve off the road onto the shoulder and tip over in the sand.

The driver just lay there laughing as we got off our bikes and approached him, telling him he was under arrest. As Bill approached him the driver jumped up and charged Bill, trying to head-butt him. Bill just stepped to the side, and our suspect fell and continued laughing. He then jumped up and charged me, trying to head-butt me, and again fell to the ground as I stepped aside. Our suspect was a good-sized fellow, six feet two, two hundred pounds. Bill said, "Enough of the bullfighting," and we grabbed the suspect to secure and handcuff him. Whatever drugs the suspect was on were working because he put up quite a struggle, not fighting but trying to pull away, with all of us ending up on the ground and him still laughing. Just as we got him handcuffed and were lifting him off the ground he yelled "Bye!" broke free, and took off running towards the river.

I started after him but Bill was already on the chase. Bill was six feet four, ten years younger, and a running back on our highway patrol football team, so I let him go. What happened next was hard to believe; our suspect ran straight onto a boat dock and jumped into the river with his hands still handcuffed behind his back. Just as hard to believe was Bill, in full motor gear, boots and breaches, gun belt, everything, diving in after him. As mentioned, there was a full moon, and I could clearly see both Bill and the suspect swept away in the swift river current, Bill swimming towards the suspect.

I knew there was a boat launch ramp about a half mile downriver and jumped on my bike hoping somehow I could assist Bill from that location. Advising dispatch of our location and situation, I drove onto the boat ramp, wanting to get as close to the river as I could, but misjudged my speed, having to lock my brakes as I skidded on the ramp, going into the river and finally coming to a stop with the water up to the top of my gas tank, red lights still flashing. I'm laughing at my own situation as I see Bill swimming towards my lights and shore with our suspect in tow, yelling, "He's still fighting me!" I yelled back, "That's because his head is underwater!" Luckily, my motorcycle stayed in place on the boat ramp with the kickstand down as I waded into the river to help Bill. We got the suspect onshore, and he spit out some water and started laughing. Bill was exhausted but looked at my motorcycle half underwater and started laughing. I was thinking about the reports we'd have to write, and soon I've joined in laughing. Just about then a couple of car officers arrived to assist; they looked over the situation and joined the laughter, especially after getting soaked while helping me get my motorcycle back on dry ground. My motorcycle started right away, with no damage from the unexpected immersion.

The real humor started at the jail as Bill and I were booking our suspect and writing reports. Other officers heard of our adventure and knowing, everyone was okay, started the ribbing: "Most of us wait until we're off-duty before we go swimming!" "Heard you tried to turn your motor into a jet-ski?" Our motorcycle breeches were 100 percent wool, and as they were drying while we were at the jail, they were also stinking, as wet wool does, and also shrinking, as they're designed to be dry-cleaned, not soaked in water. By the time we left the jail, the breeches had dried and shrunk to look like a pair of tights, and now the razing really began: "What time does the ballet start?" "Hi, Peter Pan!" We also got strange looks as we arrived at our motel to change uniforms, the breeches having to be cut off. The rest of the shift was dedicated to cleaning our weapons, trying to dry out and salvage our motorcycle boots and other leather gear, shining brass, plus doing a throrough cleaning of a motorcycle, river water still in the saddlebags.

Our suspect pled guilty to numerous charges and was fined and given thirty days jail time. He was also ordered to pay restitution for two full Arizona Highway Patrol motorcycle uniforms. Our suspect laughed when sentenced, telling the judge it was worth the stories he could tell. He then got serious and turned to Bill, thanking him for saving his life. He told the judge he realized the danger he put the officer in and was sorry for his actions. It still amazes me how Bill was able to not only save our suspect, but also swim in full motor gear, with his motor boots filled with river water like two buckets, plus the weight of a gun belt, weapon, and other gear. Bill just blew it off. "Just another night working the river."

Chapter Eight
Why Am I Here?

The late afternoon sun was setting behind the mountain ridges, its light reflecting off the water of the Colorado River. On any other day, it would have been a scenic picture that would justify me taking my eyes off the road to marvel at its beauty for just a moment, but not that day—not then. This particular seventeen-mile stretch of highway was rugged and full of dips and twists that could pose a danger to anyone who wasn't paying attention, and I couldn't afford to avert my attention for a second. Hanging onto my motorcycle, I maneuvered the twists and turns with experienced ease while trying to close the distance between myself and the red pickup truck ahead.

Lights and sirens activated, the driver knew I was in pursuit, but it appeared he was bound and determined to lose me. The hot air pounding my face, I stayed with him, just close enough behind to see him veer to the dotted line before overcorrecting and skidding off the shoulder. Back in the center of the road, the driver fought to stay on course but lost to an unanticipated twist that sent his pickup in flight. Airborne at more than sixty miles per hour, his truck flew over the sand before gravity sent it crashing, creating a billow of sand that momentarily obscured my vision of the truck. When the dust settled, its steel underside was facing the sky, heaving slowly from one side to another, before settling into its final resting place.

Grabbing my radio, I let dispatch know that the chase had ended, driving with the other hand as I made my way closer to the crash. Suddenly, I caught a blur of green to my side, and before I could react, it had struck the side of my bike, sending me launching into the air, my bike tumbling end over end at my side. Everything turned white—the noise, the sky, the sun, and the sand—and then I smacked the ground with an abrupt force. Barely registering what had just happened, I tried to move my body but was only able to slightly lift my head before my cracked helmet dropped onto the ground once again and everything went still.

Not aware of anything that was happening around me, I drifted away . . . I seemed to be somewhere else and found myself surrounded by a bright light. In the distance, I watched my daughters laughing, thinking how beautiful they were. Soon, they disappeared, replaced by darkness that seemed to overtake my vision, darkness that moved in from the outside, growing larger and larger, while the white light in the center grew smaller and smaller until it disappeared entirely.

I heard sirens in the distance, moving in and out of my head, growing louder and then fading away before reentering my awareness once again. A man's voice interrupted the pattern, frantically screaming through the still air, "963A! Frank is dead! No pulse . . . He's gone!"

Strange voices weaved in and out of my head as I fought the darkness only to find the light too bright, too blinding to allow it in. Still, I knew I couldn't succumb to the blackness—I needed to let them know they were wrong. Why were they saying I was dead? Why couldn't I see anything? What was going on? Internally, I was screaming, "What do you mean, 963A? I'm not gone! I'm right here!" But the words wouldn't come. Then there was nothing.

Suddenly, something soft and wet touched my lips, and my chest swelled with a push of incoming air before it escaped through my nose. Again, my chest filled to capacity, and I exhaled again. Soon, I took a breath of my own and was greeted with the sweet smell of flowers. As my eyelids struggled from their weight and managed to open ever so slightly, I saw golden hair framing a pretty face that was just inches from my own. I felt a soft hand on my forehead and fingers in my hair as her blue eyes came into focus and I began to make out her features.

Her face came and went, flashing on and off in my mind, each image encompassed in an intense white light. I fought to reopen my eyes while desperately trying to formulate a coherent thought. But it was useless; my head was filled with words, seemingly random, that were incapable of grouping together to create any meaningful thought. Even if they could, I couldn't figure out how to get them from my head to my tongue.

As I fought to say something, anything, I was surrounded by commotion. Realizing that any attempt to talk was futile, I tried to listen, concentrating hard to decipher what was going on around me. The noise was overwhelming, and nothing made any sense at all, but then a voice suddenly broke through the fog.

"He's back! She brought him back!"

The accident had occurred in the Parker, Arizona area, across the road from an ice cream parlor, a quaint little shop along the highway. It was owned by a man and his wife, who was a former emergency room nurse. Daphne, as I later learned was her name, had heard the sirens and seen the red truck and the two motorcycles in its pursuit. The sounds of the crash sent her running out the door, rushing to give aid, where she did what came naturally. Without hesitation, she threw her body on top of me and began CPR. For more than three minutes she pounded her fists into my chest, stopping long enough to breathe life-saving air into my lungs. It was then that I woke up—my fingers tingled, then throbbed, and I became aware of an incredible pain in my back that, like a puddle of water, oozed out into every limb. Every inch of my skin burned as if it was on fire, and I became aware of an unbearable pounding in my head.

To me, she was a beautiful angel. Staring into my eyes, she willed me not to give up and insisted that I was going to be okay. Her comforting presence never left my side, staying with me until the emergency crew was ready to take me to the hospital.

As they carried me on the stretcher, I saw a familiar face—the face that belonged to the voice that had radioed in my death. Officer Cecil Waddell, who had been the first to respond to the scene, was now reporting to dispatch that I was alive. Lying on my back on the stretcher, I listened to the communication while looking directly up into the sky, and for the second time that day I noticed the setting sun, just as the last ray was disappearing on the horizon. My mind was becoming clearer, and my thoughts were beginning to make some sense, if only I could find a way to translate them into words.

Where's the guy in the red truck? Is everyone else all right? Is my motorcycle okay? Why is it getting so hot? Don't inform my family. Don't tell my girls. Where's Bill Whitlow?

Thoughts like these drifted in and out of my mind as we made our way to the ambulance. Bloody hands to my side, I struggled with recall to answer my own questions. To no avail, my last thought before the ambulance doors swung open was *God, please let Bill be alive.*

Strapped to the stretcher, I couldn't turn my head or see, but I could hear, and a familiar voice brought tears to my eyes. Bill. Bill Whitlow, my partner and my friend, stood waiting for them to roll me into the ambulance. He had been driving the other motorcycle when we were chasing the pickup.

"That was one hell of a wreck," he said, concern in his eyes. "Are you okay, Frank?"

Moving to get a glimpse of my partner, I summoned up a small smile and somehow managed to answer. "I'll be better if you tell me you caught the son of a bitch."

"I got him."

He had him, all right, and before I knew it, I was looking him in the face. There, on the stretcher next to me in the ambulance, was the guy we'd been chasing. I noticed he was bleeding, but it was his vacant eyes and dead expression that caught my attention most and filled me with anger. The guy was drunk—so drunk he wasn't feeling anything, not even pain.

"What the hell is this guy doing riding with me? Let this asshole wait for the next ambulance," I shouted, surprised at the strength of my newfound voice.

I knew I wasn't being professional, but I didn't care. I was filled with rage—hell, the guy had literally just killed me.

Lying next to the drunken lunatic that had landed me in a chauffeured ride to the nearest hospital, I didn't know what I felt the most—anger or pain. I was becoming increasingly aware of pain in virtually every limb and part of my body from my head to my toes. I knew the guy next to me was hurt as well, but I couldn't conjure up any sympathy for him at all—just relief that he was off the streets. Tonight, anyway, he couldn't hurt anyone else.

After arriving at Parker Community Hospital, I was wheeled into the emergency room—an area so small that it was pushing it to call it a "room." Again, I found myself side by side with another stretcher—this one also carrying a motorcyclist—and by the looks of him, he had it worse than me. He had long dark hair that was wrapped in a blue bandana and was wearing leathers that were literally torn to shreds. I found myself wondering just how much skin he'd have left if he hadn't been wearing them. His face was a mangled mess that was more than difficult to look at, but it was the words that came from his mouth that were most vile.

"Hey, look at the big tough cop who wrecked his bicycle," he said, leaving traces of spit on his whiskered chin. "Serves you right," he spat. "You shoulda died out there. There'd be one less pig on the street."

If I'd been able to move and had one less ounce of integrity, I would have jumped off the stretcher and finished off what was left of his face. But I couldn't move, and I knew that letting the guy get the better of me wasn't going to do me any good. So I focused on the one thing I could do right then—survive.

Shock was setting in, and it was taking all of my strength to fight it. The urge to sleep was overwhelming, and I fought to keep my eyes open. When the effort became too great and my lids began to fall, a nurse shook my arms. Mongo, as I dubbed the outlaw motorcyclist next to me, also kept me awake with his persistent shouting and obnoxious remarks. I figured it couldn't get any worse; then they proved me wrong by wheeling in the drunken kid I'd been chasing before the accident and parking him on my other side.

Too busy trying not to pass out, I didn't care anymore, but I was relieved when a doctor approached and wheeled me into another room for X-rays, out of sight of my emergency room roommates.

The doctor explained that the X-rays revealed that I had a fractured skull. Wheeling me back into the room, again between Mongo and the drunk truck driver, the doctor said, "Let's get you cleaned up."

Out of the corner of my eye, I spotted my sergeant and the department's secretary, Kitty, standing to the side. Kitty rushed forward and held my hand, squeezing it and telling me I was going to be all right. They were a sight for sore eyes and gave me something to look at besides the bright overhead lights, but I was still fighting traumatic shock. Thank goodness for the two drunks who were doing a fine job keeping me from sleeping. By now, one was beginning to sober up, grumbling incoherently, while my friend Mongo demanded attention.

"Hey, Doc! Get me outta here! Screw these other guys—take care of me!"

Leaning down, the doctor whispered in my ear, "I'm going to give you a shot in your arms, legs, and hands. Just play along."

"C'mon, asshole, fix me up!" Mongo screamed, only to be ignored by the doctor, who swiftly and adeptly inserted a needle into my skin. The pain immediately disappeared, replaced with a welcome numbness that forbade any feeling or sensation whatsoever.

The doctor pulled out a washbasin and scrub brush. With his back to Mongo, he looked at me and said, "This is going to hurt a little, but you're an officer—you're tough, right?" Taking his wink as a cue, I replied, "Sure," only half-heartedly playing the game.

Starting with my legs, the doctor swept the wiry brush over my wounds, scrubbing them hard and rinsing the rock, asphalt and dirt into the basin. Mongo watched in silence as the hard brush turned my skin red, then purple. Making him witness what was coming his way next not only shut him up, but you could literally see the fear in his eyes.

I didn't say a word—I was enjoying the welcome relief from feeling anything. My entire body was numb, and as far as I was concerned, that wire brush could have been made of soft down feathers.

"Boy, officer. You're tough." Mongo had obviously suddenly attained a newfound respect for the law.

"Now it's your turn," the doctor said as he disinfected the

brush. "Watch this," he mouthed my way before turning his attention to Mongo.

"Okay, now. Let's see if you're as tough as the officer."

Digging the brush into Mongo's angry and swollen road burns, the doctor didn't have to wait long for a reaction. Mongo let out one of the shrillest screams I'd ever heard.

"I thought for sure you would handle the pain better than the officer," the doctor said.

Then it was my turn.

"What—does it hurt? Can't you take the pain? I thought you were the tough guy."

For good measure, the doctor dug the brush in deeper the next time, and the next. He continued until he couldn't take any more of Mongo's screams. Putting the brush down, he then turned his attention back to me and began dressing my wounds.

After four hours, my hands, arms, and legs were cleaned and bandaged. The doctor smiled, telling me that I was going to be discharged. Normally, he said, a patient in my condition would be admitted for observation and to make sure I stayed awake. However, Parker Community Hospital was a small operation, with only a few patient rooms that were usually used to hold patients until they could be transferred to a larger city hospital. They operated on limited staff and were not equipped to handle the hundreds of cases that walked or were wheeled through their doors during Easter break. For those reasons, I was released to my motel room, with the understanding that I'd receive doctor and nurse visits while I was there.

"I'll take care of him," Kitty quickly offered.

"Just make sure he stays awake all night so he doesn't go into shock," the doctor instructed Kitty. "And Frank, you'll need to see your personal physician for follow-up."

As I was being moved from the bed to a wheelchair, the old Mongo had made a comeback. Apparently, he'd survived the good brushing he'd received at the hands of the doctor and was ready for round two. "Why the hell does *he* get to leave?" he shouted.

Little did he know, but soon I'd be asking myself a similar question—with just one small change in wording: Why did I get to *live?*

Chapter Nine
What Goes Around Comes Around

Whether it's considered a privilege or a curse, once or twice in life something happens that makes us pause and contemplate the meaning of our existence. It could be an illness, a birth or death, an accident, a job change or loss, or even the end of a relationship. Regardless of what happened or why, life changes pose an opportunity for us to review our life through a different lens. Sometimes, what we see in the past and present can open our eyes to things that we've never experienced or considered in our future. The accident gave me plenty of time to contemplate my life.

When I worked at Motorola, I'd wanted a more exciting job, and being a police officer didn't disappoint. After graduating from the academy, I was assigned to a car squad that patrolled the highway between Yuma and the Mexican border. Veteran officers provided me with advice and lessons on how to be a cop—not by running checks for stolen cars or felons, but by asking the right questions and using common sense. With good training and intuition, I ranked high in felony, drug, and DUI arrests. Our particular stretch of highway was high in fatal drunk driving accidents because people used it to return home to Yuma after partying in Mexico. I also developed a nose for detecting marijuana—so much so that my fellow officers teased that I had been a drug dog in a former life. Stopping a van for a broken headlight, I seized more than three-quarters of a ton of marijuana, which set a record for uniform seizures that held for several years.

There was more to being a police officer than arresting people, though. Ironically, I was also arrested. One night while working the midnight shift, I received a report of a stolen vehicle that was headed south toward the Mexican border, which was a daily occurrence. I got lucky and spotted the vehicle outside of Yuma and activated my lights and sirens, but the driver wouldn't stop, knowing that once he crossed the border, he was safe. I radioed dispatch, asking them to contact U.S. Customs at the border and alert them that I was in pursuit of a stolen vehicle. I specifically requested that they block the entrance road to Mexico with their new heavy-duty stainless steel inspection tables. The tables had been bought to replace their former plywood tables, which had become stained from pregnant mothers, who waited at the border until they were ready to give birth and then jumped across the line to the States, where their child would be born on the ground—literally on U.S. soil. Given the unsanitary conditions, the customs workers would lift the mother onto the plywood inspection tables and assist them in the birth of their child. Over time, the wood became so stained that they could not be cleaned, which instigated the purchase of the stainless steel tables.

Customs obliged. However, the driver didn't see the stacked tables until it was too late. At a high rate of speed, he crashed into the tables and rolled his vehicle. Able to escape, he crawled out of his vehicle and ran toward his target—the white line that designated the border and his one chance for freedom. On his heels, I managed to tackle him, and after a brief struggle, had him handcuffed and under arrest. As I rose to get up, a .45 pistol was pointed directly at my face and an angry Mexican Federal Police officer was yelling at me in Spanish. Not knowing what was going on, I turned to the customs officer, who was waving frantically at the line. During the foot chase, I had unknowingly crossed the border into Mexico by three feet, and as a result, I was under arrest for invasion. The driver of the stolen vehicle was released, but my weapon was confiscated, and I got to spend the night under guard at the local police station.

Meanwhile, the customs officer alerted the highway patrol to my predicament. My supervisor came to the border to facilitate my release, but the Mexican police refused his entry into their country. The next morning, the local FBI agent (who also happened to be my next-door neighbor) came to my rescue. He had authority to enter the country on official business and was able to get the charges against me dropped. I was being released back to my country; however, my gun and gun belt were not and remained in the permanent custody of the Mexican officials.

The incident earned me a wonderful letter of commendation, which was also accompanied by a not-so-wonderful letter of instruction, informing me to exercise better judgment of distance and to stay out of Mexico. That letter was accompanied by a lot of razzing from my fellow officers.

What goes around comes around, and it didn't take long before the last laugh wasn't on me. A few months later, I was again working the midnight shift when I observed an oncoming vehicle swerve across the road and crash. Arriving at the scene, I saw that the vehicle was actually a Mexican Federal Police car and learned that the driver was the commander of the Mexican Federal Police—the same guy who told his officers to hold me overnight for invasion of Mexico. Quite intoxicated (and presumptuous), he ordered me to drive him to the border and release him. Unfortunately for him, he was in my country now, and I was calling the shots. I promptly arrested him for drunk driving, handcuffed him, and booked him into jail. He wasn't afforded the courtesy of being held in an office—instead, he was placed in the drunk tank by deputies who were all too aware of my arrest. I couldn't think of a sweeter revenge.

* * *

In early 1974, I was asked to apply for the newly formed motorcycle unit, and if I passed the training course, I would remain in the Yuma area on motorcycle patrol. I completed motorcycle training and returned to patrol duty in the Yuma area. In late 1974, I was advised I had been selected to be a member of a ten-man tactical motorcycle unit that would travel the state of Arizona on special assignments; however, the assignment would require me to transfer to Phoenix. My supervisors advised me that the transfer would be a good career move, and after giving it some thought, I accepted the transfer.

The sale of our house in Yuma was again very profitable, allowing us to purchase a nice home in Tempe, Arizona. My wife decided to return to the workforce and obtained a very good position with the Mountain Bell Telephone Company. We settled in to our new home and community, and for a while, life was pretty good. My new position required constant out-of-town travel, spending two to three weeks away from home. Again, my absence had an effect on our marriage, and we separated a couple times. Even though we tried individual and joint marriage counseling in an attempt to revitalize our marriage, it didn't work, and we ultimately divorced.

My ex-wife moved to Ohio, where her parents lived at the time, and took our children with her. I found myself reliving my father's life, wanting to be with my daughters and a part of their daily life but not being able to see them. The girls came to visit me the following summer and said they wanted to stay with me. I was a single dad for a year, which was an adventure, the young girls taking on the duties of housekeeper and cook as much as they could, given their ages, only eleven and nine years old at the time. The following summer, the girls went to visit their mother and, similar to my childhood, they were not allowed to return to Arizona. Both girls got settled in school in Ohio and made friends. Not wanting to put them through the back-and-forth custody battles I'd experienced as a child, we agreed as a family that the girls would remain in Ohio during the school year and spend the summers with me. As much as I missed my daughters, the arrangement worked. Most important, though, our kids didn't become victims of our divorce, and because we had an amicable agreement, they adapted quite well.

* * *

When my wife and I first separated, my motorcycle partner, Skip Fink, was also going through a divorce. We both had mortgages and car payments as well as kids who needed to be taken care of. Both Skip and I found ourselves financially strapped and needing a place to live. The Arizona Highway Patrol had a policy discouraging bad debts or calls from collection agencies, actually making them cause for termination. Knowing that, we approached our district commander and informed him of our financial difficulties and that we were doing our best to take care of them. It was our hope that coming forward would be viewed favorably and our commander would cut us a little slack.

At the same time, we were scheduled to start our summer patrol duty in the Sedona/Oak Creek Canyon area, where we'd work for two weeks straight, then have one week off, for the entire summer. Knowing our circumstances, our commander offered to let us work in the canyon all summer, where we'd not only receive lodging, but a daily meal per diem, as well. It was a good deal that allowed us to devote all of our salary toward bills.

A couple years before, motorcycle patrol officers rose in public popularity with the debut of a television show called *CHIPS* about two California Highway Patrol motorcycle officers. The show became a hit and its characters, Ponch and Jon, gained fame as handsome young superheroes on motorcycles. While patrolling the campgrounds and picnic areas in Oak Creek Canyon and the Grand Canyon, we received a friendly reception, and kids would often wave and yell, "Hey CHIPS!" as we drove through. People saw us as our likeable TV counterparts and often stopped and asked us questions about the local area, what to do, places to go, etc. In prior years, we had received frequent invitations to join some of the campers and picnickers for lunch, but we had always politely declined. Considering the fact that our per diem only covered one meal a day, Skip and I now reasoned that if we patrolled the campgrounds during the lunch hour, we might just get some lunch offers. And it worked. Soon, we were being asked to join campers for lunch. Sometimes, they'd pack a picnic lunch for us and let us take it with us. We took advantage of this so often that instead of the Forest Service guys calling us Ponch and Jon, they started referring to us as Yogi and Booboo, the cartoon character bear and his sidekick that were notorious for swiping picnic baskets from campers. The names stuck and word travelled. Before long, it wasn't unusual to hear dispatchers advising deputies that Yogi and Booboo needed a transport after an arrest, instead of properly identifying us as Motor 1091 and Motor 940.

Another celebrity impacted the motorcycle officers in the Arizona Highway Patrol, though if you were to ask many of them, they'd deny it. In the seventies, Joe Namath, superstar football player for the New York Jets, admitted wearing women's pantyhose under his uniform on cold game days. Given the fact that the temperature on winter mornings in the rural Arizona desert was usually in the low thirties and the wind-chill factor made it seem five to ten degrees cooler, some of the highway patrol officers decided to follow his lead and purchased dark queen-size pantyhose to wear under our motor breeches. We were surprised to find that they were actually warmer and more comfortable than thermal underwear while being less restrictive, and many of the motorcycle officers began wearing them. As you can imagine, wearing a pair of women's pantyhose wouldn't go over well with the car guys, so it became a secret that we motorcycle officers kept very closely guarded.

One day, after working an early morning shift, Skip and I were riding side by side, *CHIPS* style, as we were trained to do, when an accident ahead caused traffic to slow down. Skip yelled, "Pancho, slow down—swerve right!" and he swerved into the emergency lane. Not knowing the hazard, I barely had time to react and had just started maneuvering my bike to the right when I was hit in the rear by an elderly woman who wasn't paying attention and hadn't slowed down. The force of the impact pitched me off my motorcycle, which was run over by her vehicle. The sudden stop on the pavement knocked me out and peeled away some of my skin. Within minutes, two highway patrol cars were at the scene, and Skip, being the take-charge kind of guy he was, had me loaded into a patrol car and followed me to the nearest emergency room.

As a female prep nurse began cutting off my uniform, I called Skip to my side. Whispering into his ear, I told him to get the nurse out of the room and that I wanted him to take my uniform off me. Reassuring me that everything was okay, Skip told me to relax. Again, I repeated my request, this time with more urgency. Skip looked at me, trying to figure out what my problem was, then burst out laughing. Whispering into my ear, he giggled, "You're wearing pantyhose today, aren't you?" I nodded yes just as the ER doctor entered the room with an entourage of scrub nurses.

Again, Skip took charge. A large mountain of a man, he ordered everyone out once, then twice. With his second command, they knew he meant business and left us alone. Skip then proceeded to take my uniform—and pantyhose—off, and he even thought to hide the pantyhose deep inside the toe of my boot before telling the medical crew they could come back in. The prep nurse returned, asking why they'd been told to leave, but Skip shrugged her off, saying it wasn't important. Then, he made his exit and returned to investigate the accident.

My secret was safe, but I forgot one thing. Any time a police officer is injured and treated at a hospital, a nurse takes inventory of his belongings, including his uniform and any damage they had to do to it in order to treat the officer. The ER nurse was making small talk, lightening the situation while she inventoried my uniform, saying it looked like I would be getting a new shirt and breeches. Then she picked up my boots, commenting that it was a shame that they had to be cut off of me. Suddenly, she noticed something inside.

I saw her reach down into the toe, and just as she pulled out the pantyhose, my blood pressure and heart monitors started beeping like crazy. While she was laughing so hard she had tears in her eyes, I couldn't do or say anything. After all, it's kind of difficult to be macho when your nurse is holding your pantyhose. I was at her mercy and knew it. I begged, I pleaded, I promised her half of my retirement if she kept my secret safe. We were both laughing when the ER crew came back into the room and the doctor commented that I must not be hurt too badly, and I watched as the nurse swiftly shoved my pantyhose back into the boot. After being treated, I was sent home with a concussion, a few scrapes, and what was left of my pride.

I was so relieved that the nurse had agreed to spare me from an onslaught of humiliation that I sent her flowers and a box of candy. As far as I knew, my secret was safe and the incident would never come back to haunt me. But I was wrong.

After being off for two weeks to recover from my injuries, I returned to work to find a wrapped gift on my desk. Several of the guys from the motor squad were standing around watching as I opened it. Inside were three pairs of black pantyhose, courtesy of my ER nurse. Skip was laughing so hard he nearly fell to the floor, but was able to contain himself just enough to tell the rest of the guys the story. Soon, the whole squad room was roaring with laughter. I'll admit I took some friendly teasing from them, but they weren't too hard on me, considering the fact that most of them were also wearing pantyhose. As a side note, though, some good did come out of the incident—it became an unofficial policy that whenever an officer wearing pantyhose had to go to the hospital, another officer would accompany them to cut off their uniform.

Sometimes, though, it's the public who finds themselves in . . . let's say, uncomfortable positions. One day while Skip and I were patrolling the Oak Creek Canyon, we noted what appeared to be an outlaw motor gang ahead of us. As we grew closer, it became evident that they were members of the Dirty Dozen Motorcycle Club, which has since morphed into Arizona's chapter of the Hell's Angels. While the Dirty Dozen rarely gave us any trouble, we hung back and observed to make sure there weren't any problems.

That's when we noticed the couple on the last bike. He was swerving all over the road while he was driving. His passenger, a female, was sitting on his lap facing him. Both were naked. Realizing they were having intercourse, we pulled them over, and I received quite a reception from the woman. She was screaming at me using every cuss word in the book before she finally finished with, "One more mile, all I needed was one more mile!" I turned to my partner, Skip, who once again was almost on the ground, he was laughing so hard, and she got off the bike . . . without even a stitch of clothes on. Skip settled down, then he got her settled down, and the two bikers got dressed. After a few questions, I ascertained that the driver hadn't been drinking and wasn't on drugs, so I let him go with tickets for improper lane usage, failure to control, and, for lack of a better citation, improper passenger position. By now, we all saw the humor in the situation and were all laughing, even the driver, who said his infractions were worth the tickets. They even returned to their original position on the bike and posed for a picture . . . dressed, of course.

Arizona Highway Patrol -Days Past

Chapter Ten
Work and Mortality

As police officers, our jobs are to protect and serve. Sometimes it's a mundane job, each shift consisting of countless traffic stops and speeding tickets. But there are also times when an officer responds to life-and-death situations where they have the sole capacity to change or save a life. Sometimes we're out there to protect people from others; sometimes, to protect them from themselves. Sometimes we succeed, but unfortunately, sometimes we don't.

I was a member of a ten-man fatal accident team for the Phoenix area. The initial training we received was excellent, consisting of a two-week accident reconstruction school and a month-long course at Arizona State University School of Engineering in aircraft accident reconstruction, with the same dynamics used in car crashes. We were also sent to numerous other schools and seminars. Since I was on the motorcycle traveling squad, whenever I returned to Phoenix, I would be put on twenty-four seven call-out for the Fatal

Squad. Needless to say, dealing with death on an almost daily basis took its toll, especially when children were involved. We get used to death but always have trouble handling the death of a child. But sometimes, good things happen.

I was working motors on a two-week detail in the Sedona/Oak Creek Canyon area in early May. It was still cold in that area at that time of the year. My partner Bill and I had just completed investigating an injury accident in Oak Creek Canyon and were getting ready to ride up to Flagstaff for follow-up at the Flagstaff hospital when the dispatcher advised us of a weather warning for Flagstaff, with heavy snow expected later in the evening. Clearly, it was not a place or situation well suited for motorcycles. The highway out of Oak Creek Canyon is narrow with a series of switchbacks, very sharp corners, and sheer drop-offs, with speed limits of fifteen to twenty-five miles per hour. Over the years, I had investigated several fatal accidents involving cars and trucks going over the side. As we rode toward Flagstaff, climbing from five thousand feet to seven thousand, it got very cold, with heavy dark clouds off in the distance. We mentioned we really needed to get moving in order to complete our investigation and get out of the Flagstaff area and back to the lower Sedona area where our motel was located.

As we reached the top of the canyon, we both heard a loud crashing sound ahead of us and instantly knew an accident had occurred. We rolled up on a single vehicle accident, noting that the vehicle had left the road and hit a massive pine tree head-on. Unfortunately, in this case, the pine tree won. When we pulled onto the scene, the rear tires of the car were still spinning. In the wreckage, I saw something I had been dealing with on the fatal accident team but still couldn't get used to. A family was in the vehicle. The husband had been driving, his wife was in the front passenger seat, and the grandmother was in the right rear seat. When the vehicle impacted the tree, the man went through the windshield and died instantly. The grandmother was thrown over the front passenger seat, and in the process, she broke the wife's neck. The grandmother continued through the windshield, which decapitated her.

We set about securing the scene and calling for emergency and rescue vehicles, starting our investigation. The back seat was a mess, with coats and personal items strewn everywhere. Then Bill said he thought he heard something. Trying to get into the wreckage and moving debris, Bill yelled, "There's a little girl back here, and she's alive but really badly injured."

Motorcycle officers can only carry a limited supply of first aid supplies in our saddlebags, like a few trauma pads, wraps, portable splints, and one neck-brace—nothing compared to the larger first aid kits car officers carry with them. Unfortunately, we needed more than we had available to us.

Bill was the only one who could get inside the vehicle.

From the outside, I could only support the little girl's neck as Bill lifted her on top of the mess and applied the neck brace and what trauma pads he could in an attempt to stop her bleeding. Now that the girl was visible, we could see that she was about four or five years old. She was not unconscious but was quite dazed and didn't respond to our questions. Not knowing what was going on, she would only moan.

It always seems like forever for emergency rescue crews to arrive, but I know in reality that it takes far less time than it seems. It was no different this time as we waited anxiously for the help this young girl desperately needed. When the ambulances and rescue units arrived, they immediately removed the little girl and rushed her to the Flagstaff hospital. I told Bill to follow the ambulance and stay with the little girl and do whatever he could for follow-up at the hospital. Highway patrol car officers arrived from Flagstaff, and I stayed to help investigate the accident. It was well into the evening when we finished the investigation and the car officers advised they were leaving. I told them I was going to walk around the accident scene for a little bit—something was bothering me, like we had missed something, but I couldn't put my finger on what it could be. A good cigar always helped me think, and as the night was really getting cold, I decided to light one; it helped warm my hands as I walked around the car trying to figure it out. After half an hour, I couldn't place what was nagging my mind, so I left to join Bill in Flagstaff. Just outside of Flagstaff, it started to snow, and I received a call from the dispatcher advising that the little girl was awake. She was in very serious condition but would survive. However, she was asking for her puppy. The dispatcher asked if we had seen a puppy at the scene. That's when it hit me—when we were tending to the little girl in the back seat of the vehicle, I had noticed a dog leash, but it didn't register then—I was too busy concentrating on helping Bill apply first aid. That's what had been bothering me. The leash meant there was a dog in the car at the time of the accident.

I advised dispatch I would return to the accident scene and look for the puppy. As I drove to the scene, the snowstorm we had been advised about earlier went into full swing. As big, heavy, wet flakes stuck to the motorcycle headlight and my glasses, I had to slow down significantly to wipe off my glasses and reach around to brush the snow off my headlight. The snow wasn't covering the highway too badly but was already building up in the forest.

When I arrived at the accident scene, I had a big advantage—the snow. The snow cushioned all noise, except for the sound of it softly hitting the pine branches. I started moving in a zigzag pattern away from the accident scene, scanning my flashlight over the now snow-covered ground. My disadvantage was a barbed wire right-of-way fence, which was not fun climbing over while wearing full winter motor gear. If videoed, I'm sure my attempt would have won first place on *America's Funniest Home Videos*. But in this case, even that wouldn't have been anything to laugh about.

About fifty yards into the forest, I heard a slight whimpering. Shining my flashlight toward the sound, I saw a little black puppy shivering in the white snow. He didn't shy as I reached to pick him up, and bringing him close to my face, he immediately licked my cheek. I knew he was possibly hurt and most certainly cold. The poor little guy was shivering very badly, so I rubbed him all over to warm him up and then put him inside my leather motorcycle jacket.

The snow was really falling heavily now, leaving me with two more concerns. First, I had to get over the right-of-way fence without falling and crushing my new ward; and second, I had to get myself and the pup back to Flagstaff on my motorcycle. Neither seemed like an easy feat. It was slow going, with a few slips and slides, but luckily, just outside of Flagstaff, a highway department snowplow was clearing the highway and the city plows were clearing the city streets.

I advised our dispatcher that I had found the puppy and was en route to the hospital to reunite the puppy and the little girl. When I arrived, Bill was waiting at the emergency room door with a big smile on his face. He updated me, telling me that the little girl had serious injuries but would make it. She hadn't been told about her father, mother, and grandmother being killed in the accident, though notification had been given to out-of-state relatives who would arrive the following day. I handed Bill the puppy, which had warmed up enough that it had quit shivering inside my leather jacket. But the cold finally hit me, and I found that I was shivering so hard I thought I might drop it. As I walked inside the hospital, I was greeted by cheers, hugs, pats on the back, and kisses from several nurses and staff. Bill had been keeping them informed about the search for the puppy. He'd told them that I had found it, luckily alive, and was bringing it back to Flagstaff. One nurse approached me and offered a tray with a couple of cups of hot coffee and soup, which I welcomed appreciatively, but my shivering hampered my ability to hold onto them. I stayed behind while Bill went with one of the nurses to the little girl's room, where I later learned a great reunion between puppy and girl was had. To top it off, the nurse even allowed the puppy to stay in bed with the girl all night. Me—well, I was taken to the emergency room. My uniform was removed, and I was wrapped from neck to toes in warm towels to get my core temperature back up. As I lay there, I recall thinking that this was Montana all over again. However, an hour and several cups of hot soup and coffee later, my core temperature was near normal and I was free to leave.

By the time we left the snow was too heavy to even

consider riding motorcycles, so instead of going back to the Sedona area, the dispatchers arranged for a local highway patrol officer to pick us up and take us to a motel, where the dispatcher had arranged rooms for us. Checking in, we were each upgraded to rooms with whirlpool hot tubs. The dispatcher had told the manager of our adventure, and she said she would comp the rooms, including the upgrade. After filling up the hot tub with the hottest water I felt I could stand and putting on a thick terry robe furnished by the motel, I was interrupted by a knock at the door. Thinking it was Bill, I opened it and was surprised to see Lynn Kennedy, one of the highway patrol dispatchers who had been working the accident with us that night. Lynn was the daughter of highway patrol car officer John Kennedy, a man I enjoyed working with through the years who worked the Cordes Junction/Sedona/Oak Creek Canyon area. John was a big man, a true cowboy off the job. Whenever we called for a back-up officer in an arrest situation, which usually wasn't available in those areas, if we were lucky and John showed up, we knew everything was going to be okay.

Lynn had called her dad during our adventures that day thinking he would get a kick out of hearing about the puppy rescue and reunion. John mentioned to her that my favorite adult beverage was Jack Daniels enjoyed with a good cigar. Lynn explained that she and the other dispatchers at the Flagstaff Highway Patrol Dispatch Center passed the hat and got me a few gifts for my extra effort in finding the little girl's puppy and getting it back to her. She handed me one gift bag, which contained a bottle of Jack Daniels. The wrapping removed from the other gift revealed a very nice cigar. I was really touched that the girls had joined together and spent their own money to buy me gifts for doing something I was paid to do, especially Lynn, who had already worked a long shift and, instead of going home, had taken the extra time to purchase and deliver these special items.

But there was more. Lynn then handed me a large manila envelope. Inside was a hand-made letter of commendation/hero award the dispatchers had typed and drawn by hand to present to me for going above and beyond the call of duty to find a little girl's puppy in a snowstorm. I had received some official awards and commendations from the highway patrol that I was very proud of, but the one these ladies gave me brought a tear to my eye. Without a doubt, this one was special, and it's one I'll always treasure. After thanking Lynn and asking her to pass on a thank-you to the other dispatchers, I was ready to crawl into the hot tub. But there was something I needed to do first. I called Bill's room and told him to answer the door in a couple of minutes. I then proceeded to fill a glass with the Jack Daniels, which I took to his room. The puzzled look on his face begged for an explanation, but this was not the time. I told him to enjoy it and I'd explain it in the morning.

Bill was a real good friend, and as I sat in the hot tub

sipping Jack Daniels and smoking the cigar, a guilty thought crossed my mind—I should have cut the cigar in half and given half to him. Comfortable and relaxing from the hot tub and my glass of Jack, I puffed away and thought, no, he isn't that good of a friend.

I had trouble going to sleep that evening, as I usually did after investigating a fatal accident. It does weigh on the mind and soul to witness death—no matter how often we're exposed to it, we don't ever really get used to seeing it. That day had been as bad as I'd ever seen, I thought, as I thought of the carnage, decapitation, and a little girl who had in an instant so tragically lost a mother, father, and grandmother. Even the Jack Daniels didn't help, but I knew that was one of the purposes it had been given to me, to get my mind off of the accident so I could sleep. But then I recalled Bill telling me about the reunion between the girl and her puppy and how he described the pain on her face disappearing and being replaced by happy tears and smiles when she held her puppy in her arms. Sleep came easy after that; sometimes bad days, even those that seem as bad as they can possible get, end up being not so bad after all.

We slept in the next morning, then had a late breakfast. The spring snowstorm had come to an end, and the streets were already clearing up. A highway patrol car officer picked us up to take us back to the hospital to get our motorcycles. I asked the officer to first take me someplace where I could buy a big box of candy and flowers. Despite the puzzled look he gave me, he complied with my request. After buying both, I asked him to deliver the items to the swing shift dispatchers when they came on duty. Of course, he was curious and asked what was going on, but I only explained that they were special. He couldn't argue that point and agreed without asking any further questions.

Arizona Highway Patrol - Days Past

Two weeks before my fatal accident, I was assigned to special patrol, along with nine other motorcycle officers, in Parker, Arizona, a small town near the border of California. Every year, Parker became the host to a three-week spring break party, an event that was always chaotic and flowing with an endless stream of booze and pot. The party of 1976 was a memorable one.

Spring break attracted students, hippies, junkies, and families from all parts of the country. Almost overnight, Parker's population increased from 2,500 to 25,000. People filled the desert basin, camping in their cars and tents and surviving on a diet that consisted mostly of beer and drugs. The sweet, sickening smell of marijuana hung in the 100-degree air—the only reprieve from the heat being the Colorado River, which was dotted with skiers, swimmers, and boaters who were seemingly oblivious to anything but fun, fun, and more fun. On the sides, kids were diving from the jagged cliffs of the Whipple and Buckskin Mountains. Climbing the mountain was risky—even getting to the smallest peaks resulted in scrapes and cuts—but the plunge to the waters below was worth it, as was the applause and admiration of those who watched.

As I was cruising the highway one hot afternoon, I noticed a horde of people standing along the highway. Along with hundreds of people in the water below, they were waiting and watching in anticipation for the next person to jump into the water. Stopping my motorcycle, I peered up the mountain, where a thin young man was climbing and reaching for the next highest rock. Suddenly, I realized what he was going to do. Perched on a ledge, he was on one of the highest ridges—one that was more than 100 feet high, and one that put the highway below between him and the water. After he struggled with and regained his footing, he looked down, and I knew he was going to do it. I quickly pushed myself through the crowd, yelling at the kid not to do it, not to jump, but knew he'd never hear me. People all around were encouraging him to complete his feat, screaming, "Jump!" while yet others, those who were sober and had a conscience, yelled at him to stop.

Taking a step forward, the young man looked down. Slurring his words, he challenged them, "You think I won't do it?" Taking a white shirt from his pants pocket, he whipped it over his head like a helicopter blade while the crowd below answered his questions.

"You'll never make it, you idiot!" yelled someone with sense.

"Don't listen to them! Make us proud—fly like a bird!" screamed a topless girl, who had the decency to turn away when I shot a look of disapproval her way.

As he perched on his toes and stretched his arms outward, I felt helpless, knowing there was nothing I could do to prevent him from jumping. The kid looked down at the road and, his mind altered from LSD, saw a river instead of the highway. I held my breath, watching as he bent his knees and sprang forward, just as if he was diving into the river. The crowd went crazy and I froze with shock as this young life jumped to a senseless death. When it was over, adrenaline kicked in as if on automatic pilot, and I managed to push my way through hundreds of onlookers to get to the boy, whose body was lying in a large pool of blood.

Some of the people gathered around gasped in shock, either at what they had just watched happening or the gruesome scene it left behind, probably both. Others laughed drunkenly, unable to care or comprehend what they had just witnessed. After the fact, there were plenty of "I told you so" and "I told you not to do it" comments, as well as some that I don't care to mention. Their opinions and remarks were too late for this young man and wouldn't change the unfortunate outcome of events. It's a scene that I wish I hadn't seen, and one I know I'll never forget.

There are some things you cannot control, some things even police officers cannot change. As motorcycle officers, we were outnumbered. We couldn't stop the drinking and drugs entirely, so we had to settle for breaking up fights, keeping the crowd contained and the surrounding communities and roads as safe as possible, and hope that everyone made it out alive. Unfortunately, that wasn't the case that year.

The remaining two and a half weeks of spring break brought no shortage of arrests. I racked up more than seventy-five arrests by myself. The charges included theft, robbery, rape, underage drinking, and homicide. It was one of the most eventful three weeks of my career, and not only because of the partiers.

On the second day of spring break, Skip and I were

patrolling the highway. As we rounded a corner, we were met with a large billow of dust—a cloud of sand—and we rushed to it, knowing we'd drive up on the scene of an accident. Just as we arrived, the dust settled and we could make out the victim—our partner and friend, Charlie, whose motorcycle had just been hit head-on by a drunk driver who had crossed the center line of the road.

I jumped off my bike and scrambled as fast as I could to get to his side. Dropping to my knees, I reached for his wrists in search of a pulse. As I stared into his face, I watched with dismay as his eyes rolled back into his head. He gasped for air, but was unable to hold it, releasing it right after intake. He was struggling to breathe, and I recognized the death rattle as he began choking. All signs indicated that Charlie was in trouble—his lungs were collapsing.

"No, damn it!" I screamed. Instinct kicked in, and I drew my hand back and slapped Charlie good and hard across the face, knocking his head to the side. "You're not dying on me today!"

Focusing on Charlie and keeping him alive, I'd forgotten about Skip until a loud shattering of glass diverted my attention. Turning around, there he was, holding his bloody fist—the fist that had just punched out the driver's window of the car that had hit our fellow officer in order to drag the guy out the window—while he was still trying to drive away. His other hand was hanging tightly to a man's shirt.

"He was trying to get away," Skip explained.

Trusting that Skip would take charge of the situation, I turned back to Charlie, whose breathing suddenly appeared to be improving. The death rattle was gone, and his breathing had picked up a pace. I knew he'd turned the corner when he looked at me and was able to focus his eyes on my face.

Lightening up the moment, if only briefly, I teased, "You're lucky you responded to that hit, because if I had to do CPR, you might have had to die." I'd often teased Charlie about his long, bushy mustache and prodded him often to trim it, to no avail.

Thankfully, my remark produced a smile, albeit a small one. It was a good sign.

It took a half hour for the ambulance to arrive. In the meantime, I bent over Charlie to shield him from the hot sun and, using a towel, covered his elbow so he wouldn't look at the broken bones protruding from it. Charlie was transported by air to a hospital in Phoenix, and we later learned that the accident had crippled his arms for life.

The driver of the car was drunk, and I left Skip to tend to his arrest. It was just one of many arrests Skip had made in an attempt to get drunk drivers off the road so they wouldn't kill anyone.

In the early morning hours of February 18, 2000, I received a phone call of another accident involving a drunk driver. It was the dispatcher, who related to me a call that I'd never thought I would receive. Skip Fink had been working a midnight shift, and a drunk driver had rammed the rear of his patrol car. She informed me that Skip's car exploded, trapping Skip inside. I needed to go to the hospital right away. I made it just in time. My friend and partner Skip Fink died a few minutes after I got to the hospital. I was one of the pallbearers at his funeral. Skip had dedicated twenty-eight years of his life and career to getting drunk drivers off the road. Ironically, in the end, it was a drunk driver who killed him.

Skip (left) and I out together

Spring break and its craziness doesn't wait for injured officers, though. It goes on and on, without skipping a beat or reflecting on the dangers or repercussions of the actions of those who are participating in the non-stop party. We still had a job to do, and because of accidents like Charlie's, we were determined to do it. We didn't look too far for an excuse to get a drunk driver off the road.

Late one night, my partner Bill Hansen and I were on patrol when we encountered a car with a busted headlight, a seemingly minor infraction, but one that gave us the signal we needed to pull the car over.

Approaching the driver, we asked him if he knew why we'd pulled him over.

"Yes, sir. My headlight," he responded.

We asked him to exit the vehicle and stand behind the car. He obeyed, stiffly climbing out the door and walking with slow, sluggish steps to the back of his car.

"Have you been drinking?" I asked as the young man rubbed his bloodshot eyes.

"I drank one beer, sir, but I'm not drunk. I'm just very tired. I worked a really long day."

With that, we were obligated to run a field test for sobriety, and he passed without any problems. While following our orders, I noticed that he even seemed to become more alert and aware. It was obvious that we weren't looking at a drunk driver but instead what was referred to as a "sleeper," or someone who was struggling to stay awake while driving. Normally, sleepers would be asked to catch a nap at a nearby motel, stop for a while to get some coffee and food at a restaurant, or even stand outside in the freezing cold—whatever it took to wake them up enough that they could drive to their destination. But it wasn't freezing on this particular night—the air was hot and heavy, the kind of air that zapped the energy from even a well-rested person. We had to come up with another plan.

Trying to figure out what to do, I asked the driver for his identification. He pulled out a military ID and a Louisiana license, advising me that his name was Poindexter in a heavy southern accent that was so thick it was difficult for me to understand. I called it "mush mouth," but Bill had grown up in Louisiana and had no trouble deciphering the marine's words.

I set about explaining the dangers of a broken headlight to the young man, while Bill's practiced eye performed a quick routine scan of the interior of the vehicle, where his eyes rested upon marijuana seeds in the ashtray.

Again, I turned to Poindexter, asking him if the seeds belonged to him. He denied it, explaining that the car wasn't his and that he had just borrowed it for the night. A quick check on the vehicle's registration verified his story. Just as Bill was emptying the seeds from the ashtray into an evidence bag, a timely gust of wind whipped across us and blew them into the night. I looked over at Poindexter; there was no denying the relief that swept over his face. I had to agree. A possession of marijuana arrest would have destroyed this man's military career, a move that didn't seem justified at the time. This man didn't need to be in jail—he needed some sleep. But first, we needed to make sure he stayed awake long enough to safely get to a bed.

"Get down and give me fifty," I ordered, explaining that I wanted to make sure he was awake and alert.

Without argument, he dropped, and in true military fashion, executed perfect pushups, counting each one out loud. "One, sir . . . Two, sir . . . Three, sir."

After fifty, and creating a nice little puddle of sweat on the ground below, he snapped up and stood at attention. "Is that all, sir?" he loudly yelled, as would be expected when responding to an officer in boot camp.

Smiling, I admired the young man and answered, "That's all for tonight."

"Thank you, sir," he replied, then climbed back behind the wheel, relieved that he'd gotten through the encounter with only fifty pushups. I felt quite confident that sleep wouldn't come for him anytime soon.

Sometimes, there are things we can change and people we can help. Sending one young man safely on the road, alert, awake, and clean record intact, reminded me that there are many good people out there . . . and I was happy to be able to protect and serve them if I could. If that's what I was meant to do, for the time being, it was enough.

Chapter Eleven
Why?

As promised, Sarge and Kitty drove me to the motel from the emergency room after my near-death experience, and for the first time, I was happy to be there. Home at the time was a motel room—a temporary place to stay while I was working in the location. When we pulled into the parking lot, I noticed that the *e* was still missing from the sign, and it made me feel good. Everything was the same; most important, I was still alive.

My sergeant and Kitty helped me out of the back seat and into a wheelchair. They wheeled me through the door and put me straight to bed.

"Take good care of him," Sarge told Kitty before walking out, leaving the door open behind him. It was policy for cops to leave the door open if a female was in the motel room to discourage any allegations of hanky panky . . . not that I was in any condition to consider such a thing. As soon as he left, Kitty turned her attention to removing my bandages and cleaning my wounds, then wrapping me back up again.

She kept her word. Sitting in a chair, every time my eyelids began to get heavy and fall, threatening sleep, she'd say my name or tug at my arm. I knew it had to be difficult for her to stay awake as well and noticed that she sat very straight in her chair to avoid becoming too comfortable.

Kitty and I had worked together for some time and had developed a good working relationship. Well, I teased, and she took it well. "Why didn't you brush your hair today?" or "Where did you get those shoes—the Salvation Army?" It was all in fun, and she'd respond with a good-natured laugh, followed by a pile of reports dumped on my desk. Picking one up, I'd noticed it was a mess, loaded with typos. She'd give me a second or two for a shocked reaction before handing me the real report—corrected and polished and ready to go.

Kitty came from a family of policemen. Her father had been a highway patrol sergeant and her uncle had been director of the Arizona State Highway Patrol. She was young, only twenty-three, but had already been working at the department for six years. Everyone who knew her knew that she took her job very seriously, which was why I enjoyed kidding around with her.

Tonight, though, we didn't tease. We didn't even talk. It was all we could do to stay awake. After a while, though, the effects of the shot the doctor had given me wore off, and the pain took over. Any movement whatsoever sent searing pain through my veins, so I stayed as still as possible for the rest of the night. Instead of trying not to sleep, I tried to concentrate on something other than the nearly intolerable pain.

Kitty left the next morning, when it was safe for me to actually close my eyes and enjoy the welcome relief that sleep provided. I stayed in the motel room for three more long days that were only broken up by the television and visits from Kitty, who stopped by to bring me meals, see how I was doing, and keep me company.

The highway patrol aviation unit had several aircrafts at the time, one of which was a Queen Air, which was assigned to the governor. When the governor was not using the airplane, it was used for other highway patrol functions. After the doctor advised that I could be transported back to Phoenix, my sergeant called for the Queen Air to fly me home, thinking it would be easier on me than making the four-plus-hour drive in the back of a patrol car with a cage and no room to stretch out. He was advised the Queen Air was on standby for the governor, who might want to use it, and our helicopters were also tied up on missions. The governor, not a favorite with the highway patrol, wouldn't release the aircraft, even when he was advised it was needed to transport an injured officer. My sergeant learned that the governor's limo, which is driven by highway patrol officers as part of his security team, was going to be passing near the area. An ingenious man, my sergeant arranged for me to ride to Phoenix in the limo, with plenty of room to actually lie down on the back seat. During the ride to Phoenix, I fell sound asleep and didn't wake up during the entire trip. Also during that time, my bandages came loose, and blood got all over the back seat. I learned that the limo was put out of service for a couple of days to get the seat replaced and that the governor was really mad. Grinning from ear to ear, my sergeant said it wouldn't have happened if the governor had released the aircraft for my use, especially since we learned that he didn't use it that day at all.

Once I arrived home and Kitty and the other officer helped settle me in, I went to bed and slept some more.

* * *

A storm was looming as I came around the corner, and an unexpected ball of fire flared before my eyes. Ominous clouds overhead threatened to cloak the desert in blackness. I got off my bike and stared into the angry, rumbling sky, the hot wind in my face. The blaze I thought I'd seen grew further and further away, tucking itself behind the clouds until all I could see was a speck as it became one with what was visible of the sun.

Then nothing. No noise—no wind—no fire.

I turned and admired my bike, then threw my leg over her seat and pulled back onto the road. The clouds picked up speed, seemingly moving faster than my bike, at the same time dropping down and hanging directly overhead, threatening to swallow the desert whole with their next loud rumble. My eyes stung from the wind and the sweat, and I shook my head from side to side, hoping to move the clouds out of the way. Refusing to budge, they taunted me, forcing me to look straight into them. Suddenly, I was flying through the darkness, although I didn't feel like I was moving—everything else was. The desert below grew distant, and I fought the clouds to stay in flight, but I was no match for their anger and was thrown with a vengeance into something so hard it took my breath away. Then pain, nothing but pain as I lay there, unable to move. Looking up, I noticed that the sky had suddenly become a blinding white, only to immediately turn a deep impenetrable black as it fell from above, aiming directly for my face.

My eyes shot open in terror, and I tried to catch my breath. White-knuckled, I clutched my sweat-covered pillow so I could hold onto something until the fear subsided. I turned to look at the clock; it was four in the morning. This time, I had almost made it through the night. Relieved that morning was near, I closed my eyes one more time, hoping to get an hour of dreamless sleep before the sun rose.

The days were long, but they were tolerable. The nights, just as long, were all the same—the dream, the same. My injuries had left me exhausted, my body in dire need of sleep, but I dreaded the nightmare. While I didn't understand it, I knew that it left me absolutely terrified.

After six weeks, I had to get out of the house. I had to go somewhere or do something to break up the monotony. The reception I got when I walked into the department wasn't entirely welcoming.

"What are you doing here?"

I wasn't supposed to be back, and I knew it. I hadn't been cleared to return to duty, but I have to admit, it felt good.

Surrounded by the concern of my fellow officers, I explained that I had just stopped in for a bit to get caught up on some paperwork. I sat down at my familiar desk and started going through the piles. It felt good to have something to occupy my time. After a couple hours, Dr. Barber, the department's psychologist, popped his head over my cubical wall.

Standing up to shake his hand, I teased, "Hey, Barber, what nutcase are you visiting today?"

"I heard about your accident. How are you doing, Frank?" All business, the concern in his voice showed just how serious he was. Obviously, light-hearted banter wasn't in the works.

"Yeah, it was one hell of a wreck," I admitted. "But I can't stay home doing nothing all day, so I thought I'd come in and tackle some of the paperwork that's stacking up."

"Are you staying on motors when you come back?"

"Of course," I replied without hesitation. "Gotta get back on the horse, you know."

I still had six more weeks of recuperation and recovery before I'd be cleared to return to duty, which would give me more than enough time to consider my options. But there was no question in my mind—I was a motorcycle highway patrol officer, and that wasn't going to change.

He asked me to follow him into an empty office and have a seat. Barber had never been anything more to me than a friendly acquaintance, but it didn't take me long to realize that this visit was more than just friendly conversation. As I gave him details about the accident, he listened and studied me closely. He talked to me like a friend, but listened like a doctor. It seemed he knew all the right questions to ask to draw me out and get me to share even more. When I got to the part where I mentioned death, he took a slow deliberate sip of his coffee and sat straighter in his chair, taking a keen interest in my responses. I felt comfortable talking to him and tried to adequately describe what it had been like—the black tunnel, the circle of white light, the sensation of flying while waiting for the dreaded moment that I'd hit the ground.

These were things I had tried not to think of during the last six weeks, things that I'd pushed into the recesses of my mind. Now, they were coming forward, and I found that reliving them was difficult. At times, I was overcome with emotion and had to close my eyes, wanting to shut off the memories, while also trying to get a clearer picture of them.

"You realize you died that night, right?" Barber's voice softly pulled me back into reality. "Many people experience what we call the 'tunnel.' You're one of the lucky ones who survived to talk about it."

I hadn't felt lucky . . . After all, I'd been in a very serious accident. I had died. But suddenly, I got what he meant and realized that I was lucky. Police officers know that their lives are at risk every day, but they don't think about it. I never really thought it could happen to me. But it did. Dying was no small matter, and I had a lot to think about. As Barber followed me out of the building to my car, one question was already weighing heavily on my mind.

Why was I spared?

I was grateful that I was given the time and opportunity to find the answer.

Chapter Twelve
Stumbling for Answers

I spent the next six weeks in serious thought. Why was I here? What was I meant to do? What, if anything, was I supposed to learn from the accident? The answers didn't come. However, by accepting what had happened instead of pretending it hadn't and pushing it back into my mind, something did happen—a sense of peace and acceptance replaced the nightmares and frustration. I knew I didn't have the answers and that it was impossible to will them to come—but they would come when the time was right. I had to accept that and move on with my life.

Don't get me wrong—it wasn't easy. I had to deal with a lot of frustration, mostly with myself, for not being able to heal faster. I grew irritated when I couldn't do things as well or as easily as before. You might say I was more than a little impatient. You definitely could say I was not the best patient.

Kitty, however, had enough patience for both of us. I appreciated how thoughtful and caring she was—it was a side of her that I wasn't often exposed to at the department. She visited, even though she didn't have to, always reminding me that it was going to take time before I fully recovered, while also being just stern enough that she wouldn't allow me to feel sorry for myself for even a second. It took a while to heal after the accident. There was extreme pain for a few weeks, especially when it came time to change my dressings. I've never been a fan of pain medication, so I avoided taking any if at all possible. The skull fracture resulted in nausea and dizziness, but in my case, I also suffered from a loss of motor skills. I sometimes had difficulty walking, picking up things, and getting dressed. From time to time, I had to concentrate to remember where things were—like the bathroom.

I was ready to go back to work . . . and not afraid at all to get back on my bike. Even more exciting, I was told that I was getting a new motorcycle since mine had been totaled in the accident. There is a connection between a motorcycle patrol officer and his bike, and when there's an accident, it's not uncommon at all when one of the officer's first questions is "How's my bike?" I remember that once I'd recovered my ability to speak, it was one of the top questions weighing on my mind, along with "Is my partner okay?" and "I hope they got the bad guy."

This time after my accident was a period of healing and transformation. My marriage officially over, I wrapped myself up in work, which was nothing new for me . . . and in many ways one of the main reasons for the demise of the marriage. I missed my daughters but saw them every chance I got.

I truly enjoyed being around children, so it seemed only natural to use my career as a way to help them. The motorcycle squad I was on was assigned at the time to work special details throughout the state of Arizona, assisting with traffic control in smaller towns, cities, and counties. Again due to the popularity of the television show *CHIPS*, young children weren't afraid of us, and they frequently called out to us, asking us questions and showing interest in our motorcycles. Whenever we were assigned to a specific area for a week or more, my partner and I would contact the local grade school and ask permission to visit the school and teach them bicycle safety. It became a well-received program—the kids loved the chance to sit on our motorcycles and play with the sirens and lights, while the administrators, teachers, and parents appreciated the safety lessons we provided.

My work with children expanded, and soon I was helping with Special Olympics events. It became a way to give back, and I really enjoyed the time I spent with the kids when I had the opportunity. To me, it was important that children knew that police officers weren't the "bad guys"—that we really were there to help them, not only as officers of the law, but as members of their communities. I enjoyed developing positive relationships with the children and being a role model they could look up to and turn to, rather than being afraid of.

In the meantime, I worked patrol, helping with traffic control, which could include anything from directing traffic for parades and other events to DUI stops and checks. It was routine work, but being a cop, there were always unexpected moments and requests.

It was a typical morning. The alarm clock started its relentless beeping at 4:00 a.m., waking me up so I could get ready to work the day shift. After packing up my gear, I left my Phoenix home and headed into the desert. I remember it well—the air was rather chilly that April morning, and it felt refreshing and energizing. Everything was still and quiet as I cruised down the Beeline Highway, taking in my surroundings as the sunrise was replaced by blue skies. It was one of those days when everything seemed perfect, so much so that it even crossed my mind that today was going to be a special day.

Admiring the scenery, I was interrupted by a radio dispatch.

"Can you copy a 10-21 number?"

Code for telephone, I pulled over to the side of the road. "Go ahead," I responded.

"Can you find the nearest 10-21 and call Detective Ron Cox?"

It wasn't the first request of its kind I'd received. In fact, it was quite common. So was driving another twenty to thirty miles to find the nearest payphone. I wrote down the detective's phone number and turned my bike around and headed back to Phoenix, where I placed the call from the first payphone I encountered.

That's when I learned about Chris. Detective Cox gave me some background, a little boy who had leukemia who was nearing the end of his fight. Chris had a dream—he'd always wanted to be a highway patrol motorcycle officer, just like his heroes Ponch and Jon on the show *CHIPS*. Ron explained that he wanted to make this little boy's dream come true, and he wanted my help.

This little boy's story tugged at my heart, and I instantly knew that I'd do anything I could to give him one special day. Ron explained that he'd gotten permission from Chris' mother, Linda, and his doctor for the boy to ride from the hospital in Scottsdale to our department in the DPS helicopter. Knowing the work I'd done with school children, Ron said he thought of me and asked if I could meet the helicopter when it landed and show Chris my motorcycle.

"I know how much you love working with kids," he said. "I thought you might like to be there to greet Chris and show him your bike."

"This has to be a special kid, since he loves the *CHIPs* officers," I commented. "How'd you hear about him?"

"His mother, Linda, goes to night school with the wife of U.S. customs agent Tom Austin," he explained. "When Tom's wife found out that Linda's son dreamt of becoming a highway patrol motorcycle officer, she told Tom, and he told me. So what do you say, do you want to do it?"

"Sure, I'd love to meet him," I said without hesitation.

Hanging up the phone, I jumped back on my bike and drove back out onto the highway to department headquarters. Along the way, I had a lot of questions. Not knowing what to expect, I wondered what this little guy, Chris, would be like. Just how sick was he? Would he able to walk? Would he be sad?

It didn't take long to find out. That afternoon I waited, along with fellow officers, commanders, and other employees, at the DPS headquarters in Phoenix. The helicopter blades chopping the air announced their arrival. Figuring he'd be brought out in a wheelchair, I was surprised when the door opened and a pair of sneakers emerged. Out stepped Chris, an excited seven-year-old who seemed so full of life it was hard to believe that he was sick. He skipped down the steps and ran right toward me, smiling the whole way.

Sticking out a long, thin arm, he giggled. "Hi, I'm Chris."

Bending down so I could look him in the eye, I shook his hand.

"Well, hi, Chris. I'm Officer Frank."

I put Chris on my motorcycle, and it was obvious he was in awe. His feet dangled on the footboards, while his fingers rushed to push every button and switch he could find. He impressed me with the fact that he knew what they were all for as he beamed with delight when he activated the lights and siren.

"Neato!"

Chris' mom stepped forward to introduce herself.

"Hi, I'm Chris' mom, Linda. Thank you so much for doing this for him. I haven't seen him this energetic and happy in a long time."

"It's our pleasure," I replied, finding that I really meant it. I was enjoying giving this moment to her son.

Then, Chris looked at me with the smile of a child living his dream. "Hey, I'm Ponch and you're Jon," he said before turning his head and pretending he was driving my bike. He grumbled pretend motor sounds, even accentuating the shift in gears, and grabbing the handlebars, he turned the front wheel back and forth.

"Do you want to go for a spin around the parking lot?" I asked.

Suddenly, Chris backed off. His eyes darted nervously before he surprised me by saying, "No thanks."

Explaining that I'd hold onto him, I added, "You just flew in a helicopter. It's scarier up there."

"Helicopters have doors," Chris replied. Point taken, I had to admire his reasoning.

On cue, my sergeant, Jim Eaves, pulled up in his patrol car. I knelt down by Chris and told him I had an even better idea, but Chris wasn't paying attention. He leaned in close to me and reached out to touch the shiny wings pinned to my uniform. Tracing their edges with his finger, he whispered, "These are neato."

He lingered to admire my wings a bit longer, then

jumped off my bike to the ground. It was a good time to repeat my offer.

"Do you want to drive a patrol car? It has doors."

He didn't even answer. Without a word, he took off running toward my sergeant. Using both hands, he pulled the heavy door open and jumped inside, hopping right onto Jim's lap. Chris then grabbed the steering wheel and once again pretended he was the driver, while Jim struggled to get the seatbelt strapped around both of them.

"Do you want to push the pedal, or do you want me to?" Jim teased.

"You can do it. But can I steer?" You could hear the hope in his voice.

"You sure can," Jim said. Chris pulled himself closer to the steering wheel, ready and waiting for the car to go into motion. They slowly drove around the parking lot, and when they passed me and a fellow officer, Chris looked right at me and smiled, then turned his bubble gum into the biggest bubble I'd ever seen. When it popped, it left its sticky pick residue all over his face, which Chris thought was hilarious. His laugh shook his whole body.

"That's our Bubble Gum Trooper," I said. Watching Chris so happy and energetic, I nearly forgot that he was sick. When I remembered the reason for this visit and that Chris had a terminal disease, I had to fight to control my emotions.

Chris wasn't sad—he was ecstatic. He was out of the hospital and living his dream. He was living each day, each moment, to the fullest. Watching him and gaining so much respect for the huge soul inside this small body, I knew it wasn't enough. There had to be something more I could do for him.

At that moment, they came to a stop in front of us, and Jim told Chris they were going inside the department for a special surprise. Chris was all eyes as he and his mom were led through a maze of hallways, past the squad room, and into the office of our chief, Colonel Richard Shafer.

"I'm glad to meet you, Chris." Colonel Shafer stood and shook his hand. "I understand you want to be a highway patrol officer. I think we've got some things that will make that happen."

Colonel Shafter placed a camel-colored Arizona Highway Patrol hat on Chris' small head. Its brim overpowering most of his face, he lifted his face and smiled, just as the colonel handed him a seven-point badge.

"To be a police officer, you need your own badge," the colonel explained as he gave Chris the bright gold badge that had the words Arizona Highway Patrol etched around the state seal.

Chris stared at it in awe, twisting the bright gold star to watch it shine as it caught the light. Knowing what to do, Chris held it up to his windbreaker, and the Colonel officially pinned it on him. With a sense of wonder, Chris gently rubbed the badge, a moment his mom was catching on camera.

"Wow," he said, obviously starstruck.

From there, Chris was taken to the office of Ralph Milstead, who was director of the DPS at the time. When the handshake and introductions were done, Chris kindly offered Ralph a piece of gum.

"I see you have a hat and badge, so now we're going to make you a *real* highway patrolman, Chris," Ralph announced, handing Chris a certificate identical to the certificates officers received when they were sworn in. Of course, Chris wasn't sworn in, but the certificate made him an honorary officer with the Arizona Highway Patrol—the very first and only honorary officer in the department's history. With his hat, badge, and certificate, in Chris' mind, he was a real patrolman.

"Does this mean I'm a real officer?" Chris asked, his voice simultaneously full of hope and joy.

"It sure does," Ralph assured him. "You're one of us now."

There was a lot of pride in the department that day—while Chris was busy being a very proud little trooper, his mom's pride shone in her eyes every time she looked at him. My fellow officers and I were proud that we could do something to make a difference in their lives. For a while, it had been easy to forget his prognosis, but as Chris became weary from so much excitement and had to leave, we were reminded that he was very ill. It was incredible, though, to see how much joy he found in life, as well as how much joy he brought to others.

That evening, I learned that Chris was doing so well that his doctor had released him so he could spend the night at home. He wasn't at the department anymore, but he hadn't left my thoughts since the moment the helicopter took him away. There was no doubt that we'd brought happiness to our little seven-year-old Bubble Gum Trooper, but I wanted to do more and was glad when Ron brought it up on the phone that night.

"Why don't we have a uniform made for Chris?"

"That's a great idea," I agreed. As long as Chris was an official officer, he should also look like one.

Putting the wheels in motion, Ron contacted the seamstress who made all of our uniforms. Once she heard Chris' story, we didn't have to convince her—she began working on his uniform and stayed up all night to finish it. We picked it up the next morning. A miniature version of our official uniforms, it was perfect, and we couldn't wait to present it to the newest member of the force.

I led the procession of highway patrol motorcycles and squad cars to Chris' home in Scottsdale. Lights activated and sirens screaming, we drove down Chris' street and pulled into his driveway, capturing the attention of neighbors who peeked out their windows and walked out onto their driveways to see what was going on. Chris also heard us, and by the time we arrived, he was standing at his front door watching with amazement. The uniform hung from its hanger in all its glory as Jim handed it to Chris.

"Go ahead, try in on, kid," Sergeant Eaves said as Chris took the uniform and ran back into his house. In hardly any time at all, he came back, walking so proud and tall, and wearing both his uniform and one of the biggest smiles I'd ever seen.

"Can I get on the motorcycle?" he asked.

Not feeling a need to reply, I lifted him up and placed him on the seat, then switched the radio to a frequency that could contact every officer in the state. "Announce that you're on duty, Chris."

"Good mooooorning, Phoenix!" he yelled. His voice came through the radios of every officer standing in the driveway and echoed up and down the street. Chris was surprised when dispatch responded, "Good morning, Officer Chris. I'm marking you 10-8," code for "on-duty."

"How do I become a motorcycle cop?" Chris asked me.

"Well, we'd have to set up training for you, but you don't have a bike."

I barely got the words out of my mouth before Chris jumped the motorcycle and ran into the house. Before we had time to wonder what was going on, he came back out riding a battery-operated police motorcycle, which I later learned his mom had bought for him in place of a wheelchair.

"Will this work?" Chris asked, his mom standing by his side.

Not only had Chris brought out a motorcycle, but he

also carried a helmet and a pair of black boots. He had all of the gear necessary for training and really looked like an official motorcycle officer, minus his small size. We got to work placing orange cones on the driveway to create a makeshift obstacle course, and Chris promptly jumped on his motorcycle and began maneuvering it. As we watched, his mom shared that when Chris felt well, he used to drive his little police motorcycle up and down the street, placing tickets on all the cars that were parked by the curb. Laughing, I realized that not only had Chris dreamt of being a cop one day, he'd been one in heart for a long time.

It was an honor to watch Chris successfully master his motorcycle training. He was taking this very seriously as he gripped his handlebars and was all business as he came to a stop in front of me. Turning his bike off, he didn't even ask if he'd passed, but the question he did ask had me fighting back tears.

"When do I get my wings?"

It took me a minute to compose myself, but I promised him he'd get his wings very soon. As we visited for several more minutes, it became obvious that Chris was getting sleepy and it was time for us to let him get some rest.

After leaving Chris' house, I drove straight to Apache Junction—I had a promise to keep. All of our wings were custom made, and I had to talk to the jeweler to request a special pair for a little boy whose time was far too short. Again, after hearing Chris' story, the jeweler promptly got started and spent the night casting a new pair of shiny wings. The next morning, he called to tell me they were ready. I can't describe the appreciation my fellow officers and I felt for everyone who went out of their way and worked together to make Chris' dream a reality, and I was speechless when the jeweler told me there was no charge for this very special set of wings. As I tried to express my gratitude and tell the jeweler how happy he had just made one little boy, he patted me on the back. Sometimes, the greatest payment you can ever receive is knowing you made a difference in somebody's life, especially when it's a sick child.

As I left the jeweler, there was just one more thing I wanted to do—I called NBC. It was a long shot and one that probably wouldn't pan out, but I explained who I was and shared Chris' story, then requested an autographed picture of Ponch and Jon, the motorcycle patrol officers on their show *CHIPS*.

The pictures arrived a day later. As I was getting ready to take the photos and wings to our little trooper, my phone rang.

"Hi, Frank. It's Ron. I just wanted to let you know that Chris is in a coma at St. Joseph's Hospital. The doctors don't expect him to make it through the day."

Oh no. I wasn't prepared. My heart dropped at the news, and a lump quickly filled my throat. As I shut my eyes to fight back the tears that threatened to fall, Chris' bright smile flashed through my mind, and I managed to pull myself together. I'd promised our little Bubble Gum Trooper his own set of wings, and I was going to do everything I could to make sure he got them. Not wasting a minute, I grabbed them and the autographed pictures and rushed through traffic to get to the hospital. Rushing to Chris' room, I had to pause and prepare myself before opening the door. Taking a deep breath, I quietly pushed it open.

Chris lay in the hospital bed, his body looking so small and still. His mom was by his side, holding his hands and crying as she looked down at her son. The beeps of the monitor told me that Chris was still alive. So frail and pale, he didn't look like the little boy I'd grown so fond of in the last few days. It was as if the life had already gone out of him, taking with it his cute little grin and bright blue eyes.

To the side hung his uniform, as tiny and neat as it had been when we handed it to him just a few days before—everything was the same, everything but Chris. I walked over to the bed and bent down to hug Linda, who somehow found the strength to thank me for coming. Overcome with sorrow and speechless, I walked over to the small uniform and officially pinned the tiny wings on the uniform shirt. As I snapped it closed, Chris squirmed. With a groggy voice, he asked, "Am I an official motorcycle cop now?"

"You sure are," I said, not even attempting to hide the tears that were falling down my face. It was one of the hardest things I'd ever done, but I had just fulfilled the last part of Chris' lifelong wish.

Quickly, while Chris was still awake, I pulled out the autographed pictures and handed them to him. He stared at them for a few minutes, soaking it all in and admiring his television heroes, before he finally spoke. "Thank you, Officer Frank."

"You're welcome, Chris," I replied.

It was an extremely emotional moment. Linda was leaning over the bed, her arms stretched out as she sobbed and cradled her young son. Her tears fell freely, landing on Chris' pale cheeks, but even so, I was able to see him smile. What a brave little boy, I thought as I smiled back one last time. It was time for me to go, and I squeezed Chris' cold hands and said my goodbyes.

Humbled by the enormity of the situation and overcome by sadness, I realized I'd only known this remarkable young boy for a short time, but the impact he had made on my life was immeasurable. When I got the news that he had passed away later that evening, it took my breath away. Squeezing my eyes shut to stop the tears that threatened to spill, I reminded myself that Chris was in a better place—a place free of pain, and doctors, and hospitals. He was now free of his diseased body and could fly with the unbridled joy in which he had lived his life.

Our little Bubble Gum Trooper had earned his wings in more ways than one. Smiling through my tears, I hoped that the wings I'd presented him with helped him fly a little higher.

Chris the Bubblegum Trooper

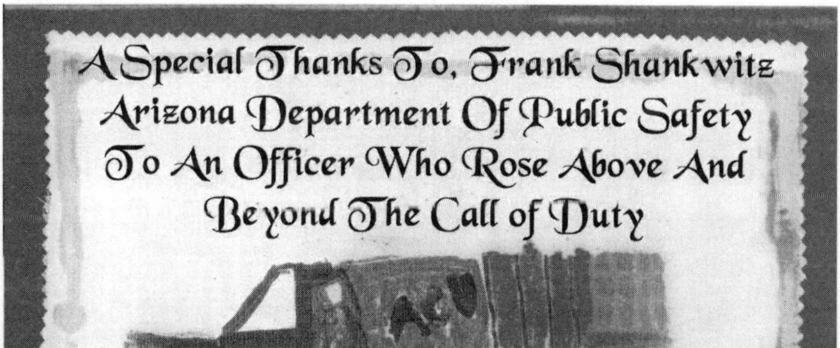

A note from Chris

Chapter Thirteen
Proper Goodbyes

After Chris passed away, I was called into the office of the director of the Arizona Department of Public Safety. Director Milstead advised me that as far as he was concerned, we had lost a fellow officer. He learned Chris was going to be buried in a small town in southern Illinois and asked if I and another motor officer would go to Illinois to attend the funeral and give Chris the proper honors of a fallen officer. He advised it would be an off-duty assignment, and I would have to use vacation time and cover my own expenses, but he would authorize permission for us to be in uniform. He also advised he had started the steps to collect donations to cover our expenses.

It seemed such a small thing to do, but to me, it quickly became a priority to make it happen, especially when I heard that his funeral was being held in Illinois, where Chris had been born and many family members still lived. It was something he and I had in common that I hadn't known.

The biggest obstacle was figuring out how to raise enough money for airline tickets, given such a short amount of time. Another officer suggested passing a hat around the department, and by the end of the day, we'd raised half of the money we needed from our department, as well as from other departments and police agencies throughout Arizona. Still, though, we were short $780. The next morning I was brainstorming, trying to figure out how we could raise the money in time to get to the funeral, which would be held in two days, when the phone rang.

"Office Shankwitz," came my usual and automatic greeting.

"Hey, Frank—it's Jerry."

"How ya doing, Jerry?" I asked.

Jerry and I had known each other for years. A local helicopter reporter for an NBC affiliate, he covered many of my fatal accident investigations. Over time, we'd become friends.

"I'm doing good," Jerry replied. Then he moved quickly on to the reason for his call. "I heard that you're trying to raise money for the little boy. How's it going?"

"Well, yesterday we raised enough for one plane ticket. We're still working on raising enough money for the other one."

"Frank, come down to the studio and I'll help you out."

I obliged and went to the station that afternoon, believing that Jerry was going to make an announcement on television. Thinking that he might actually put me on air, I quickly straightened my shirt and fixed my hair before getting off the elevator. I was rehearsing what I'd say when the elevator doors opened into the station's lobby.

I was greeted by the receptionist, a brunette with a nice smile, who somehow recognized me as soon as she looked up from her typewriter.

"Yes, that's me," I said, watching as she reached for a long white envelope that had my name on the front. I opened it right there, surprised to see a personal check from Jerry in the amount of $780, along with a note, "Take care of the little officer. I would have blown this money on a blonde, anyhow."

Laughing, I placed the envelope and its contents in my pocket before thanking the receptionist, who informed me that Jerry was out of the office at the moment. After letting her know that I'd be back to thank him personally, I rushed back to the department.

* * *

Tickets purchased, Officer Scott Stahl and I drove through small towns on the outskirts of Chicago. Originally, Bill Hansen was supposed to accompany me to Chris' funeral, but at the last minute, he couldn't make it. Like me, Scott had grown up in Illinois, so he was the logical choice to take Bill's place. After landing, we drove to Chicago and visited my father and then to Joliet, where we spent some time with Scott's parents. Surrounded by farms and cornfields, the small Midwest towns blended into each other, one after the next, as we made our way to Kewanee, the small town where Chris' funeral would take place. On Interstate 80, a quickly growing and busy interstate that had replaced the old two-lane road my dad used to take to Kewanee when he had overnight business, we were making good time, and Scott and I passed some of it talking about Chris.

Scott had never had the privilege of meeting our little Bubble Gum Trooper, so I brought him up to speed, sharing the little boy's stories and the time we'd spent together.

"What a brave little boy he was," Scott commented, as touched as we all had been when we met Chris and learned his fate.

"He sure was. He had a better outlook on life than most healthy children I've met. It makes you wonder, though, why sometimes a child so young has to die," I replied, staring out the window and shaking my head. It just didn't make sense. "I'm just glad we were able to do something for him while he was still here. We owe him this funeral."

As we drove along Interstate 80, my mind traveled back to my childhood and the occasional summers I traveled to Chicago to visit my father. It wasn't long, though, before my thoughts were interrupted by familiar flashing red and blue lights streaming through the Jeep's windows, accompanied by the wail of a siren. I looked over at Scott, who seemed half asleep, and moved to the side of the road.

"I wonder what this trooper wants. I know I wasn't speeding," I remarked. A little irritated at the inconvenience, the irony of being pulled over by the police lightened the moment and I laughed. "I liked it better when we were the only car on the road."

Rolling down my window, I watched in the mirror as an officer from the Illinois State Police walked up to the car. Placing his hand on the roof, he bent down to peer inside. Knowing protocol, I kept both hands on the steering wheel in plain sight.

The officer didn't waste any time.

"I stopped you to find out what two guys wearing Arizona State Police uniforms are doing driving a Jeep through Illinois."

Ah, yes, our uniforms—we were dressed for Chris' funeral. It was a legitimate question and one I might have asked if the situation was reversed. After all, it's not an everyday occurrence. The Chicago Police Department knew we were here and why—in fact, they had sent an officer to pick us up at the airport and take us to my stepbrother's house. It was my stepbrother's Jeep that I was now driving to Kewanee—but this trooper had no way of knowing that. I quickly gave the officer a brief rundown, explaining why we were here.

By the time I finished, the trooper's disposition had turned itself around.

"One of our officers recently moved to Arizona to become a motor officer," he said. When he told me the officer's name, I immediately recognized it.

"Well, this really is a small world. I just finished training him," I replied.

"Get out! No kidding!" the trooper said.

After spending a few more minutes talking with our newfound friend, I told him I had to cut our visit short and asked if we were free to go.

"I don't want to keep you," he assured, "but I want to make sure you don't have any problems finding your way. And we don't want any other officers to pull you over for the same reason I did. Follow me, and I'll lead you to the end of my jurisdiction and make arrangements for another officer to take you from there."

For the next forty miles, we followed the officer. As promised, we were then met by another state officer.

"Take good care of them," the first officer said to his replacement before wishing us good luck and sending us on our way once again.

It was the third officer that met us who led us into the town of Kewanee. We followed him into a nice, quaint neighborhood lined with large, mature trees. When the officer stopped his car along the curb in front of a mile-long stretch of cars, I pulled over.

It was obvious Chris had been very loved. We had to walk more than a block to reach the funeral parlor, a rather beautiful Victorian home surrounded by green grass and occasional tree roots that had erupted through the lawn. Chipped paint on a short fence and cracked sidewalks told its age while giving it a homey feeling.

Suddenly, I stopped. Realizing I wasn't next to him and the state trooper anymore, Scott turned to see what was keeping me. My feet froze, unable to move, as I looked at the parlor, where more than fifteen police officers stood waiting. I felt a chill, which was quickly overwhelmed by tears as I realized just how much Chris had touched the hearts of so many people he'd never even met.

Wondering how these officers knew about Chris and our involvement with him, it suddenly dawned on me. *Of course, the trooper who pulled us over had done this.*

Here we were—two Arizona Highway Patrol motorcycle officers, and officers from every agency in Illinois—strangers to each other pulling together as a unit to complete the dream of one very young, very special little boy.

"Frank?" Scott asked, walking toward me to see what was wrong.

"I'm okay. I guess my emotions are getting the better of me."

Putting a comforting hand on my back, Scott walked by my side to greet the officers.

I found my voice and thanked the officers for coming. "It means so much to us that all of you are here, and I know it would have meant a lot to Chris. He would have shaken hands with and made friends with all of you by now, offered you a piece of gum, and asked for a ride in your patrol cars."

It was small talk, but it broke the ice and made the situation a little more comfortable. But still, we all knew why we were there, and the moment was solemn. One by one, Scott and I introduced myself to each of the officers; one by one, they all expressed the same sentiment—they were grateful that they could be a part of it.

Two men not in uniform then approached me. Smiling, they introduced themselves before quickly getting to the point. They each owned a Honda Gold Wing motorcycle and were offering to let Scott and me ride them in the funeral procession.

"We'd be honored if you'd use them," one said.

"We heard you had to leave your bikes behind, so we polished them just in case you wanted to lead the procession with a couple motorcycles. You're more than welcome to drive them."

Touched, I thanked them and told them we'd be honored to drive their bikes. It would be an amazing tribute to Chris. "I promise we'll take as good care of them as we would our police bikes. If you scratch up one of those, they really smack you upside the head."

Then we took a few minutes to walk to the other side of the street to see the bikes. Like the men had said, they were perfect. Beautifully polished and shined, they were ready to escort Chris to his final resting place with the honor he so deserved. As we walked back to the police officers, I saw a familiar face standing among them. It was the first time I'd seen Linda since the day Chris had passed away. She looked so small, so lost, so tired, and so very weak. Her sad eyes connected with mine, and her lips spread into a tight little smile that held back a sob, while her red puffy eyes spilled fresh, hot tears. Once she wrapped her arms around me, she wouldn't let go, sobbing uncontrollably as she clung to my uniform. Her tears were an emotional release for me, as well—and with them, I was able to swallow my own tears and feel a sense of peace. I needed to be strong for Linda, for her family . . . for Chris. I held her until she regained her composure and pulled away, thanking me through her tears for everything we had done.

"He was a special boy. He deserves this," I replied, meaning every word.

With a small squeeze of my hand, she led me through the front door into the funeral home. Although rows of people filled the chairs, the room was achingly quiet. Some were praying; others were holding tight to their loved ones. As my eyes passed over them to the front of the room, my heart started beating wildly in my chest as I saw Chris' small white face.

Finally at peace, his body rested in a wooden casket surrounded by flowers—on one side stood a beautiful bouquet in the shape of a star, sent by the Arizona Highway Patrol

* * *

Someday, when you have something to give to somebody, make sure you do.

Juan's words replayed through my head as I glanced around my kitchen table and looked at Kitty, Chris' mom, Linda, my fellow officer Scott Stahl, and Kathy McMorris. It had been nine months since Scott and I had traveled to Illinois. During that time, I'd spent the majority of my non-working hours creating the foundation. As I contemplated why we were all here and what we were trying to do, I had to give credit to Juan. His influence on my life had been strong and positive. The imprint he'd made on my life, along with his words of wisdom, had brought me to this day.

After moving to Prescott, I hadn't seen Juan for eighteen long years until one day in 1978 when I found myself on a special assignment that brought me back to Seligman. There was no way I would drive through the town without stopping to say hello to my friend. In full uniform, I walked into the Snow Cap restaurant, remembering which doorknob actually worked. Everything looked the same as I remembered, yet smaller. Right away, I spotted Juan standing behind the counter. With his back to the door while he was talking to customers, he heard the door swing shut and spun around, as he'd always done whenever someone walked in. Looking at me, he didn't say anything right

Association; the other side was framed by a spray from the Arizona Fraternal Order of Police. Linda walked by my side to view his body—resting so still and calm. Gone was the unbridled joy and awe I'd come to know; yet he had the same sweet face I remembered—a face that could grin a mile wide and blow the world's largest bubbles—a face that touched so many and showed them what it was like to love life to its fullest. His eyes closed and his voice now silenced, he looked brave and stoic, just like a real police officer, as he lay in full dress in the tan uniform we'd had made for him and that had brought him so much joy.

The time was nearing, so I respectfully stepped back to give Linda a few last, precious minutes to say what has to be the world's hardest goodbye—the goodbye between a parent and child. As she looked at the face of her son, her smile showed a bravery and courage that reminded me of Chris. But her smile was accompanied by tears—tears from a mother who was grieving the immense loss of her child. It was an emotional scene. Watching them was sad, but once again, I felt peace. I knew they were together—they always would be. Their bond wasn't broken. Chris was still there—he could see his mom, hear her, and even feel her as she gave his hand one last loving squeeze. As she looked down at her son, I knew somehow that her son was also looking down at her.

Take care, little trooper, I thought, then turned to lead his mom to her seat and take my place at the back of the room with the other officers. The service to honor the youngest and newest member of the Arizona Highway Patrol was about to begin.

Frank and Chris

Chapter Fourteen
Stepping Up

Leaning against the wall, my mind wandered away from the service. I didn't hear the words spoken during the sermon or the speeches that celebrated his short life and were intended to bring comfort to those he left behind. Instead, I thought of Chris—happy, smiling, and laughing. I saw the wonder in his eyes once again, almost as if he were standing in front of me. My mind wandered back to my fellow officers and the civilians who all came together to bring that wonder and happiness to his face. I was grateful that we were able to give so much joy to him, my only regret being that he would never know just how much he had taught me and the incredible impact that he'd made on my life in just a few short days.

Sensing that people were rising from their seat, my mind came back to the present. The service was over. Along with the other officers, we formed two rows on each side of the back door and stood at attention while the small coffin was carried between us to the black hearse. The funeral director then placed the Arizona state flag that I had brought with me over the coffin to honor our fallen comrade. Scott and I then walked to our borrowed bikes and slowly pulled forward. Ten police officers lined up behind us, with the hearse and limousines carrying the family in our wake. Slowly, we led Chris to his grave, the flashing lights from the patrol cars our silent tribute to Chris and an honor to his courage and his life.

After the prayers were said at the graveside service, Scott and I, as in military funerals, marched to the casket and, in a formal fashion, folded the Arizona state flag in the same official manner as one would fold the United States flag. When our task was complete, I approached Linda and presented her with the flag in honor of her son.

"On behalf of the governor of the state of Arizona and the Arizona Department of Public Safety, we express our condolences and sorrow in the loss of Chris, a fellow trooper," I said, once again triggering tears. I was able to hold mine back, but Linda's fell freely as she thanked me.

Escorting Chris Home

Laying Chris to Rest

After several more prayers, the service concluded. Our little Bubble Gum Trooper was laid to rest, and it was time for us to return to Arizona and leave our fallen officer behind.

As we settled into our seats for the return flight home, we were approached by a very friendly flight attendant, who asked, "Are you okay with sitting in an emergency exit row?"

After assuring her that we were, she smiled again, then paused. Wrinkling her forehead and tilting her head to the side, she stared at us intently for a moment.

"Hmmm, okay. Thank you," she said before continuing down the aisle and tending to other passengers.

Scott was the first to speak.

"That was strange," he said.

"Yeah, it was," I agreed.

The plane took off down the runway, and before we'd even climbed to our altitude, I reclined my seat and leaned my head on a pillow against the window. It wasn't long before I was asleep. Not long after that, I was awakened.

"Hey, Frank, wake up," Scott said, nudging my arm.

Startled, I shot up and opened my eyes.

"What? What is it?" No sooner did I speak than my eyes regained their focus. Standing in the aisle were three flight attendants, all staring at us.

"Aren't you the officers who came from Arizona to bury the little boy?" one asked. Evidently, her question triggered the friendly flight attendant's memory and she chided, "That's where I know you from!"

It didn't come as a surprise that they knew us, since a television station had filmed our arrival in Illinois and had also provided coverage of Chris' funeral on the news.

"Yes, ma'am, it's us." I smiled.

"The pilots and I saw you on the news when we were getting ready for this flight. We were so moved by what you did for that little boy. It was amazing," said the third attendant.

"Thank you. He was a really great kid," I said, knowing that Chris deserved more credit than I did.

"Why don't you get your things together and come with us?" This again came from our friendly attendant.

Scott and I looked at each and shrugged our shoulders, thinking *why not?* Grabbing our carry-ons, we were led through a curtain into first-class, where we were invited to sit down. As we made ourselves comfortable in the plush and spacious seats, the attendants placed nice, cozy pillows behind our heads. We were impressed with and grateful for the accommodations, and quickly thanked the attendants, while also expressing that we really didn't deserve any special treatment.

"Well, we think you do." Surprised by a man's voice, we looked up to see a tall man dressed in uniform stepping through the door at the front of the plane. "There aren't enough people anymore who do such wonderful things for children," he explained.

After shaking our hands, the pilot went back to the cockpit. As soon as he walked through the door, another man stepped out. He, too, was in clothed in an official pilot's uniform. Shaking our hands, he introduced himself as the co-pilot. It was a moment of recognition from the flight crew that caught us off guard—we never expected favorable treatment, a pat on the back, or fame of any kind. The satisfaction of knowing we played a role in making Chris' lifelong dream come true was more than enough.

While Scott napped, I stared out the window, taking in the clouds and the blue sky that stretched for miles in the distance. I was no longer tired. In fact, I was wide awake and found myself thinking more clearly than I had since Chris died. It gave me an opportunity to really think about everything that had happened, from the moment I'd gotten the call asking if I could be present to meet Chris when he got off the helicopter, to the day I gave him his wings in the hospital, and then to the funeral that honored his short but remarkable life. I was taken aback by the kindnesses that had been extended. People who had never met Chris had gone out of their way to make everything happen. The seamstress stitched all night long to create a custom-made uniform for him, and the jeweler had generously volunteered his time and services to produce a tiny set of shiny silver wings in record time. There were the actors who autographed their pictures for the little boy, countless police officers and employees throughout the whole state who contributed their hard-earned money so Scott and I could attend his funeral, my friend Jerry at the television station, and police officers in the state of Illinois who'd never met Chris, or us, but who took the time to join us in giving him a service fitting for a decorated officer. Then, I remembered the two men who had loaned their motorcycles to two complete strangers so we could lead the procession, which brought me to the present and the flight crew who had gone out of their way to thank us for doing something that had brought us just as much joy as it had brought Chris.

If I'd ever lacked faith in mankind, I didn't now. I was overcome by the compassion and generosity I'd witnessed in the last couple weeks by strangers joining together to make a difference in one little life. I thought of Chris and the joy they'd collectively brought to his last days, and my mind began to spin. Suddenly, I realized that Chris wasn't alone—there had to be other kids like him, kids who we could help. If we could accomplish such a great feat for Chris in such a short amount of time, imagine what we could do for them.

We can make wishes come true for other kids . . .

Suddenly, it didn't matter what I wanted to do. I knew what I *had* to do. In helping Chris, I had found my purpose. For the first time, I knew why I was here.

away. Turning to put his spatula back on the grill, he excused himself from his customers before he spoke.

"The mop's in the back. Get to work!" he ordered.

"Yes, sir," I replied, noting that everyone else stopped talking.

As I obediently walked toward the kitchen, all eyes were on Juan. The air was filled with questions and confusion. Had Juan really actually just ordered a cop to get to work? And why was the cop doing as he was told?

It only took a minute for Juan to meet me in the kitchen, where he proceeded to give me an affectionate bear hug. Then he stepped back and took a good long look at me, shook his head, and grabbed me for hug number two.

"It's been a long time, Frank," he said, his eyes exaggerating as they traveled the distance from my head to my toes. "You're a lot taller now."

"I guess I grew up since the last time I saw you—literally," I replied.

Laughing, we grabbed a couple metal chairs and sat down to catch up on each other's lives. Juan's questions were nonstop—where are you living? Look at you—you're a cop! How long have you been doing this? We managed to catch up on the major events in our lives and covered the highlights of the last eighteen years before I had to go—after all, I was on duty. During our visit, I noticed that Juan looked the same—a little grayer around the hairline, but the same. He still loved pulling corny pranks and making his customers laugh just as much as he loved seeing a busload of tourists pull up outside the door. This time, when I left, I promised to come back every time I came through town, and I meant it. I didn't want another eighteen or twenty years to fly by before seeing him again. Life was too short and Juan was too special to let that happen.

I kept my promise and visited Juan many times, never letting too much time elapse before visiting my friend. It was time well spent. In fact, it was Juan who inspired my next announcement to my friends sitting around the table.

"This foundation is going to become national one day, and then international."

I looked at Kitty—her eyes never wavered in doubt. The others, though, laughed, thinking I was ridiculous for having such a lofty goal.

"Yeah, right. Frank, we could hardly afford to pull off Chris' wish. What makes you think we're going to be able to grant wishes across the world?"

Chris' wish had been a challenge, but not an insurmountable one. People stepped up with acts of kindness and donations of time, money, and talents that had made it all possible—and in an unbelievably short string of time. With planning, I knew we could create something larger, something that would bring smiles and laughter to kids not only in Arizona, but across the United States and beyond.

The foundation actually started taking shape a month after Chris' funeral. My desire to help make dreams come true for other sick kids hadn't been a fleeting one—if anything, it became stronger with each passing day. I announced it first at an annual barbeque for officers—one of those "we survived another year" celebrations that gave us and our families an opportunity to let our hair down and have a little fun together.

"I want to find other children who are ill and help them to—" My words were interrupted by a little boy who ran up to the woman I was talking to.

"Mommy, look at the yo-yo my friend gave me," he said.

"That's very nice, sweetie," she said. "Now go play for a while. I'm talking to this man about something important."

"This idea you have sounds wonderful," she said, looking at me. "Please continue."

As I shared my idea with her, other people approached and listened.

"What's this I hear about you starting a foundation?" one officer asked. His wife, who had been listening as well, said, "If you ever do anything, I want to be involved. I mean it. Call me when you get things going."

That woman was Kathy McMorris, who now sat across from me in my kitchen, brainstorming ideas. We were a small group, but it was enough to get off the ground. Of course, everyone didn't jump on board, and there were people who said they wanted to be involved but who didn't follow through for various reasons. But the initial response was positive, and I knew that we could really make it work. I knew I needed help to do that.

One of the first orders of business was to determine what the foundation would do. My first official foundation document was created on a single piece of paper, where I listed four categories of wishes that, in my mind, covered anything a child could ever want—to be something, meet someone, go somewhere, or have something. It lacked finesse and legal jargon, but it was a start.

I decided that the foundation would require a doctor's permission for the child to participate and that the child's family would be included. The rest would take time to mold, but I had patience. Most of all, I had determination. I knew deep in my soul that this was why my life had been spared. It was why I was given the opportunity to come back to life after I'd died. It consumed me and my thoughts, and it soon became clear that this dream was bigger than me—so big that I wouldn't let anything stand in its way. There was no obstacle I couldn't overcome in order to make the Chris Greicius Make-A-Wish Foundation a reality.

I contacted Linda, Chris' mom, a week after the barbeque. We arranged to meet for lunch, along with Scott, at a restaurant in Scottsdale. I shared my idea with her, watching her closely and trying to read her expressions. When I finished, I asked, "What do you think? Are you on board?"

She looked at me for a moment, and when she did, I

saw Chris in her eyes. He was happy and smiling, in total agreement with my plans. Linda must have felt it, too, because right then, a smile spread across her face.

"Let's do this," she said.

The excitement in her voice was noticeable, but there was an underlying sense of sadness. She knew the reason for the foundation—it was for Chris and other kids like him, kids who were suffering, kids who were sick. While the purpose of our foundation was to bring happiness into a child's life, there was no denying that the need for it was very sad.

Chapter Fifteen
The Make-A-Wish Foundation

In creating any charity or foundation, there are legalities and formalities that must be followed, and ours was no different. If I was going to create this foundation, I wanted to do it right and make it official.

The first order of business was selecting an attorney. We needed legal advice about how to officially establish a foundation. We agreed that I'd contact Patrick McGroder III, a friend of mine who, luckily, also happened to be a lawyer.

Patrick agreed to help us and quickly took care of the necessary paperwork with the Arizona Corporation Commission. He informed me that he would take care of everything, including filing a 501c3 to make us a not-for-profit foundation. He also advised that we'd need official bylaws that would establish the logistics of the foundation and its operation, as well as a board of directors.

I was named the CEO of the foundation, and Scott became our vice president. Secretary and treasurer responsibilities were assigned, and lastly, Linda was given a special role. As community liaison, her job was to find children with terminal illnesses for us to grant wishes to.

On Patrick's advice, I sought the services of a certified public accountant and reached out to Douglas Bell, a friend who had been a CPA for many years. Like Patrick, Douglas agreed to act as our accountant and informed us that he'd take care of everything we needed.

I never realized how much work and planning went into creating a foundation or any other type of agency, and I was surprised at all of the planning and details that were required. But it was a labor of love. We trudged through the steps one by one at meetings held in our kitchens, living rooms, or an empty patrol office. Finally we had most of the logistics squared away and were ready to begin. But there was one very important component missing that prevented us from granting our first wish. We needed money.

The need for funding necessitated the need for publicity. At the time, I was working off-duty as an undercover security officer for Smitty's, a local department/grocery store, a gig I'd held for several years. Walking into work one day, Cecil, the store manager, approached me.

"Well, aren't you quite the celebrity," he said.

"What are you talking about?" I asked.

Cecil must have preferred to show rather than tell, and I followed him as he walked to the snack bar located at the front of the store. After we'd both sat down at one of the tables, he pulled out a newspaper that he'd had folded under his arm, opened it up, and laid it on the table.

"Look at that," he said, pointing at the front page of the community news section in our local newspaper, the *Arizona Republic.* One glance told me all I needed to know—the article was a special feature about Chris. The story had grown legs, and newspapers and television stations across the state had all picked it up, telling their viewers and readers about the last couple weeks of our little trooper's life.

"Pretty amazing," I remarked, awed by the attention the story had attracted from so many who had never had the pleasure to know Chris.

I went on to tell Cecil about the work we'd done to start a foundation so we could help other children like Chris. When I was finished, Cecil had just one question. "Do you have a bank account yet?"

"Well, no. We're not that far along. We're just starting to put together a fundraising campaign. We'll open a bank account when we get our first donation."

Cecil rose from his chair, and I followed him as he walked to the back of the store. Pulling a couple rumpled dollars from his pocket, he handed them to me.

"This oughta do it," he said.

In my hand were two bills, a ten and five. We had our first donation.

Touched, I thanked him. But he wasn't done yet. Cecil then opened up an account for the Make-A-Wish time, we'd known each other for nearly eight years. However, we were very careful to keep our personal relationship a secret from others in the department. One morning, our district captain called Kitty and me into his office. Apparently, he'd heard that we'd been seeing each other and threatened to file a complaint with internal affairs, which would probably result in the loss of both of our jobs. He not only threatened to do so, but already had the paperwork in hand. However, his disposition and disapproval did a complete turnaround when I informed him that I was, in fact, divorced and had been for several months. Tearing up the paperwork, a broad grin spread across his face, and Kitty and I received his official permission to date.

Kitty never got to meet my father, who passed away on April 4, 1981. Ironically, at the same time he was dying, I was saving another person's life.

I had spent the better part of the weekend in Prescott helping some of my former high school classmates plan our twenty-year high school reunion. It was early afternoon when I departed to go home to Phoenix. Traffic was moving well as I drove down the highway, then suddenly slowed to a crawl. I scanned the highway, noting that traffic was totally gridlocked in the northbound lanes, before my eyes rested on the problem. Across the median, two cars were rocking belly up in the dirt, their tires still spinning. There had been an accident, and it appeared to be serious.

At the time, I was driving my Bronco, so I didn't have

Foundation, and we promptly deposited the fifteen dollars in it. In a very short time, I'd just gotten our first donation and opened our bank account, all because of one newspaper article. It was a start, but we needed a lot more.

The rush of publicity that had been generated by Chris' story gave life to our fundraising efforts. Soon, we were receiving cards and letters, many of which contained checks or money, from people all over the state,. Within three months, we had raised $2,800, enough to grant our first wish. But there was another little snag—we hadn't yet found a child to grant it to.

Chris' mom, Linda, took care of that. After spending hours at St. Joseph's Hospital, which I'm sure must have been difficult for her, she'd found our very first Make-A-Wish child. Frank "Bopsy" Salazar was a seven-year-old boy who had terminal leukemia, much like Chris. Bopsy had one wish—he wanted to be a fireman.

Bopsy's mother, Vienna, gave me directions to their home in Guadalupe, Arizona, where I drove to meet him and hear his wish firsthand. I followed the twisting dirt roads and turns for several miles outside of Phoenix until I pulled into their driveway, where Bopsy and his mother greeted me.

The visit had been planned, but from the look on his face, it was obvious that Bopsy had not been told I was coming, or why.

"Hi, I'm Officer Frank," I said, reaching out to shake the

little guy's hand. "I'm a friend of Linda's. Do you know why I'm here?"

Never losing eye contact, Bopsy confirmed my suspicion by shaking his head. There was no excitement that would indicate he had the slightest inkling what my visit was about, just as there was no fear that a police officer was talking to him in the driveway.

"I hear you have a wish," I said.

Still, I received no response. Without saying a word, the boy continued to look in my eyes. As I reciprocated, I saw the eyes of a child who was much older than his years. I couldn't help but notice the seriousness behind them, and it crossed my mind that this child had lived a hard life. I even wondered if it was too late, if granting this child a wish at this stage would make any difference in his life at all.

"He's not supposed to show much emotion at this time," Vienna explained.

I later learned why. Bopsy was a Yaqui Indian and, at the time of my visit, had been participating in one of their religious ceremonies. The Passion and Resurrection of Christ dramatized the events in Christ's life through music and dance. Each member of the community played a different role in the ceremony, even Bopsy. However, during Lent and Holy Week, they not only played a role during the dramatization, but also in their life. Because Bopsy was devoted to the custom, he had temporarily been transformed from a playful and vibrant child to the serious and solemn boy who stood before me.

Satisfied that his lack of emotion had nothing to do with my visit, I tried to draw him out, just a little. "Come take a look at my car," I said, motioning to the police car that I'd parked in the driveway.

Bopsy hopped into the front seat, and as he gazed at all of the switches and buttons, I got a glimpse of admiration and awe. It was enough.

"If you could have any wish in the world, what would it be?" I asked.

His answer wasn't immediate. He took a few long moments before replying. But when he did reply, it was with conviction.

"I want to be a fireman."

"What?" I asked, with an exaggerated gasp. "A fireman? Why not a policeman?"

It worked. Teasing him just a little was all it took. Trying not to giggle, he pressed his lips tightly together and looked away from me for a second.

"Well, I've always wanted to ride a hot air balloon, too. And go to Disneyland," he said, avoiding my question altogether.

His first wish wouldn't be difficult at all. Since Kitty's brother was a fireman, I knew we'd be able to grant it without any problem. My mind turned to the hot air balloon ride, and realizing I had a couple friends who owned me one, I was pretty confident that we could make that happen, as well. But Disneyland? That one could be difficult.

I spent a few hours getting to know Bopsy and Vienna that day. When it came time for me to leave, we were friends.

"Did you realize that we both have the name Frank?" Bopsy asked me.

"I sure did."

"And that our name in Spanish is Pancho?" he added.

"It's a good name, isn't it?" I replied, winking as I patted his little shoulder. "Have a good night, Pancho."

Vienna's mom thanked me for coming, telling me that I had made Bopsy's day. Shaking her hand, I assured her that I would see her soon.

Chapter Sixteen
The First Wish

The next afternoon, I presented Bopsy's wishes to the board. Our first order of business was determining which wish to grant, a process that wasn't as easy as we had originally thought it would be. After going back and forth for an hour, I spoke up. In my mind and heart, the boy wasn't asking for much, so I made an executive decision, hoping the board would agree.

"We're going to break the charter already and grant all three wishes. After all, he is our first official Wish child."

Fortunately, one by one, the board wholeheartedly agreed.

"I don't see why not," Kathy stated.

"We've got the money; let's do it!" added Kitty.

From there, things happened quickly. Within a week, Bopsy was high in the sky, looking down at Prescott and Dewey, Arizona, in a bright and brilliant hot air balloon. I called to ask him what he'd thought of the ride, and he assured me it was everything he'd wanted it to be. "It was really neat. We were soooo high, just floating in the sky. Thank you, Pancho."

That did it. Bopsy had managed to tug my heartstrings, just like Chris had. My throat grew tight, and I looked up at the ceiling as I fought to hold back my tears. As soon as I blinked, the tears that spilled down my cheeks proved my effort was futile at best.

"You're welcome," I somehow managed to reply.

It was happening again. The tightness grew in my chest, as if my heart really did hurt, and I had to fight to control my breathing. Bopsy had managed to touch me deeply, and the fact that I knew he had so little time left broke my heart. I thought about Chris and Bopsy and other children like them, and the unfairness of it all was almost too much to bear. Then I realized that their lives were too short to dwell on impending sadness, and if we could do anything to bring them some happiness in their last weeks, we could give them something to look forward to and some added strength that might help them hang on just a little longer.

Making Bopsy an "official" fireman was the second wish. Just as I'd hoped, Kitty's brother, Pat Carlisle, came through and made granting the wish simple, but very special. On that day, Bopsy and his mother were given a guided tour of Station 1 in downtown Phoenix, where he also got to meet Fireman Bob, who was a funny and loveable character on a Phoenix children's television show called *The Wallace and Ladmo Show*, as well as a real fireman.

Kitty and I stayed in the background and watched as Pat introduced Bob to Bopsy.

"I'm Bob, but you can call me Fireman Bob," he said, stooping low to bring himself down to the boy's face. "You must be Bopsy."

After they shook hands, Bob led Bopsy up the stairs so he could see the one thing that every child loves about a firehouse—the pole. Standing on the ground floor, we looked up and watched Bob teach Bopsy the correct way to grab the pole, cling to it, slide down it, and, lastly, land safely. Clinging to every word, Bopsy took a few moments before he felt confident enough to give it a try, then he reached his arms out to hug the pole, wrapped his feet around it, and began his descent. At first, he slid slowly and cautiously, with his eyes on his mom who was waiting below, then he quickly loosened his grip and flew to the ground, where he was caught by a firefighter positioned at the bottom. The gleam in his eye was evident when he caught my eye for just a second, but then he took off again to follow Bob, who had another surprise in store.

"Hey, everybody, we have a surprise over here for Bopsy," Bob announced from across the station. A wide wave of his arm beckoned us over to watch as Bob presented Bopsy with a very small yellow jacket, a matching helmet, and a pair of black boots.

"This is for serving as our youngest and bravest firefighter," he said. "We're pleased to make you the city's first honorary firefighter."

When I saw the uniform, I was in as much disbelief as Bopsy. My eyes grew wide with the amount of thought and caring that had everyone had put into making Bopsy's wish come true. I had seen it with Chris and now with Bopsy as these selfless firefighters from the Phoenix Fire Department had gone above and beyond to bring happiness to a child who didn't have long to live. Any doubts I'd had about Bopsy's excitement were long gone by the time he quickly dressed in his uniform, donning his hat and boots. The television crews and reporters that had been with us all day were snapping pictures and rolling their cameras before he even had his little arms in the sleeves of his new bright yellow jacket. As the reporters asked him one question after another, he answered them admirably, with short, honest responses, but he never stopped fussing with his uniform until the last hook of his jacket was snapped closed.

Fully dressed and ready for duty, Bopsy finally looked up. To me, he looked taller, prouder, and happier than he had at any moment during the day, maybe even during his entire life. He was literally beaming.

Watching the immense joy on his face, I was suddenly overcome with just as immense sadness as my mind rudely reminded me why we were there. Placing one hand on Vienna's shoulder, I said, "I'm so happy we were able to do this for Bopsy. And I am also so sorry for what you and your family are dealing with and will face."

Her reply impressed me, and I'll never forget it . . . or the strength that it must have taken for her, as his mother, as she softly said, "He knows he has leukemia. And he has no fear of death. He knows what's coming, so he tries to live life to the fullest, one day at a time."

Again, the enormity of her words didn't escape me. Here was a young child, who should have a full and promising life ahead of him but instead was facing death in the very near future. He wasn't afraid to die, but he also wasn't afraid to live. It was such a solemn moment that had a profound effect on me, as did the silent strength I saw when Vienna looked at me and smiled. Almost in prayer, I lowered my head while contemplating what she had just said.

The sound of a horn was startling and enough to bring my attention back to Bopsy. There he was, seated in a fire truck, proudly pounding the horn with about as much delight as anyone could imagine. The driver pulled the truck out of the garage and into an alley behind the station, where Bopsy enjoyed dousing water on a few cars and winding the fire hose. When they pulled the truck back in, Bopsy signified their return in full glory by repeatedly flipping the switches, sending the wail of a siren and the circles of red light back and forth across the department.

Like the rest of us, Vienna watched intently as her son experienced this, his biggest and greatest lifetime wish come true.

"Ever since I can remember," she said, "Bopsy has been crazy about being a fireman. He has always loved the bright red colors and the sound of a fire truck roaring down the street."

"I can see that," I replied. And I truly could. There was no denying that today, we had managed to make one little boy very, very happy.

Once he was out of the truck, Bopsy walked toward us, somehow managing to keep his head held high under his yellow helmet. He was living his dream, ready to fight fires and save lives, but his mother had to take him home. While we all knew why he was there, it was easy to momentarily forget that he was still a very sick little boy. Bopsy had to go home and rest and gain some much-needed strength before receiving his third wish.

A free trip to Disneyland might have seemed like a small thing to do for a terminally ill child, and it is, but the process of trying to make it happen proved otherwise. I started by calling the public relations department, hoping that Bopsy's story would tug their heartstrings as it had mine. Every time I asked them for free admission and a tour for a terminally ill child, I was met with "We can't help you." Because I was a police officer, though, I was guilty of one thing—I didn't give up easily, and this was one pursuit I was committed to.

Of course, the employees at Disneyland had heard similar stories. I'm sure they were no strangers to people calling all of the time, asking for a discount or free admission for every reason under the sun. And I couldn't blame them for saying no. In fact, I knew that for the most part, every person I contacted probably only had the power to say no. What I needed to do was find the one person who would listen long enough to know that our request was legitimate. I needed to find the one person who had the power to say yes.

I gathered together articles about Chris and the Make-A-Wish Foundation and mailed them with my request. It took a few tries and a great deal of persistence, but finally I got the attention of someone who not only believed us, but who could actually approve the request. They called and advised Kitty that they would be happy to make the necessary arrangements to provide a tour and free admission to Bopsy and his mom. Not only were they willing and accommodating, but they, too, offered to make his wish even more special, saying, "He'll even get to meet some of the Disney characters, and they'll show him around the park."

It was great news, but there was one last detail that we had to put into place. We had to get Bopsy and Vienna to Anaheim, California. So, the very next day, I drove to Sky Harbor International Airport, where I spoke with a representative from Hughes Air West, who was more than happy to provide two free airline tickets for Bopsy and his mom. I couldn't wait to share the news with our little firefighter.

"Yeah!" he cried, followed by a slightly muffled yell as he called out to his mom, "Mommy, we're going to Disneyland!"

His reaction was all I needed to know that we had done the right thing by granting all of his wishes. Our first official wish was proving to be a success on all counts, but I wanted to make sure that it stayed that way, so I made one last phone call.

"Anaheim Fire Department, is this an emergency?"

"No, it's not," I replied. "This is Frank Shankwitz. I'm an Arizona Highway Patrol officer, and I'm also the founder of the Make-A-Wish Foundation in Arizona."

After introducing myself, I explained the purpose of my call, telling the dispatcher about Bopsy's illness and prognosis. Then I asked for a contact at the fire department who we could call just in case Bopsy became ill during his trip.

I've worked with dispatchers during my entire career and have always found them to be extremely helpful and willing to go the extra mile. She was no exception and immediately stated that she would connect me with the captain on duty.

After listening to my story for a few minutes, the captain wholeheartedly agreed to my request. "You can certainly contact us if anything goes wrong," he said with a hint of excitement in his voice. "Listen, why don't you give me his flight number and arrival time, too?"

Without asking why, I gave him the information he'd requested, but it wasn't until a few days later that I actually learned why he wanted to know. Linda, Kitty, and Allan Schmidt, a DPS public relations representative, and I drove Bopsy and his mom to the airport, where we fully intended to say goodbye at the gate and send them off. When we arrived at the gate, though, we were greeted by a couple employees from the airline. A friendly stewardess then offered to take us on a little tour of the cockpit.

"We're not actually flying today," I explained, gesturing toward Bopsy and his mother. "These are the lucky two."

"Well, if you *all* want to follow me," she repeated, "we'll give you a quick tour before takeoff."

"Did you hear that?" Vienna said to her son. "We get to see the cockpit."

Bopsy had never flown before, so he'd naturally never been in the cockpit of an airplane. It was one more special touch, like so many, that surprised us.

Bopsy and his mother entered first, while the rest of us followed and scrunched closely together to fit into the limited quarters.

"Let's see if this fits," the pilot said, and we watched yet another generous act as he placed his brown hat on Bopsy's head. Despite the fact that it covered his ears and slid down over his eyes, the pilot proclaimed that it was a "perfect fit" and told Bopsy he could take the hat with him if wanted to.

Before long, it was time for Bopsy and Vienna to take their seats. Before we left them, Bopsy tugged at my hand. Kneeling down on one knee, I looked into his big eyes and asked, "What is it, Pancho?"

In the sweetest voice, he answered my question with a question. "Can I bring you back a gift from Disneyland?"

Of course, I was touched. Here was a little boy who knew he was dying. Besides that, he was on his way to Disneyland! And here he was, thinking of *me.*

"That'd be great. I think I'd like Mickey's autograph. Will you bring that back for me?"

"Sure," he readily agreed, then turned to take his seat for his very first flight.

When they got off the plane, another surprise was in store for them, as I learned in an unexpected phone call I received later that day.

"This is a dispatcher from the Anaheim Fire Department, just calling to let you know that Bopsy and his mom got here just fine. A few firefighters picked them up from the airport in their truck, and they're heading to their hotel now . . . Hello?"

I was speechless, so much so that the dispatcher had thought we'd lost our connection.

"Sorry," I said, almost in a whisper, as I shook my head, trying to comprehend just how incredible people can really be. "Wow."

Her patience as she waited for another moment until I was able to pull myself together and find the words to respond indicated that she seemed to understand.

"Thank you so much. How's Bopsy doing?" I asked.

The enthusiasm in her quick response assured me that he was doing great, just as she said.

This act of generosity by the Anaheim Fire Department

had been unexpected. The first-class treatment they provided to our little firefighter was an awesome step up from the taxi that we'd arranged to transport Bopsy and Vienna to their hotel. From the moment the two arrived at the airport until they reached their destination, they had been given royal treatment by some truly amazing people. The fact that they were all a class act was not lost on me for a second.

Bopsy and his mom spent three days in California, where he enjoyed every minute of his third wish. People stepped up to the plate and did everything they could to make it better for them—two fireman escorted them around the park for an entire day, where they rode rides and even got a tour of the park's operation behind the scenes. Newspapers and television reporters had gotten word of Bopsy and his wish, and they followed them around, asking questions and taking pictures throughout part of a day. Then, when it was time to make the journey back home, the Anaheim Fire Department picked them up in a fire truck and, activating the lights and sirens, drove them back to the airport and saw them off.

I got the call just a few days later.

"Bopsy is very ill, and they don't expect him to make it through the next couple of days," Vienna said, no longer trying to hold back her tears.

It was heartbreaking. I sat in silence, not being able to help remembering receiving that same phone call about Chris, our Bubble Gum Trooper. Now, another wonderful little boy was finding what should have been a full and happy life cut far too short. He wouldn't live to turn eight, and he'd never get to become a real firefighter. The unfairness of it all felt like a punch in the gut, momentarily knocking my breath away.

Dutifully, I called Fireman Bob to inform him of Bopsy's condition. The very next day, I made my last visit to the little guy.

The scene in Bopsy's hospital room was strikingly similar. When I walked in the door, Chris' little face flashed through my mind, but when I approached the bed, I saw Bopsy, looking just as still and lifeless as Chris had when I'd come to say goodbye. His eyes were barely open, but he somehow managed a smile.

"Hi, Pancho." is Hh

His voice was weak and the words were slow, so different than they had been just a week before.

"Hey, buddy. How're you feeling?" I asked, not really knowing what to say at a time like this. In reality, does anyone ever know what to say to a little seven-year-old child who is dying? Again, the unfairness of it all stabbed at my heart.

"Okay, I have a gift for you," he said, looking to his mom, who opened her purse and pulled out two pieces of paper.

"I brought back Mickey's autograph signed on one of the park's programs, and I drew you a picture," he explained.

After a perfunctory glance at the autograph, my attention

turned to the picture. I gazed for a moment at the fire truck Bopsy had drawn, but it was the words he'd written below it that nearly dropped me to my knees.

Pancho: Puedo Poner la Siren, Frank?

Now, anyone would have to be made of stone not to melt, and there were more than a few tears welling in the bottom of my eyes, but I fought to contain them when I raised my head and looked at Bopsy.

"Can I turn the siren on?" he translated.

Nothing I could say, absolutely nothing, was worthy of a response. Even if my broken heart had managed to come up with a response, I wouldn't have been able to say it. Instead, I leaned down and hugged this beautiful, strong little boy with the hope that he would know just how much he, and the words he had written, meant to me. Looking over, Vienna's tear-drenched face said it all.

Then everything grew so still and so quiet as Vienna and I sat next to her child's bed, staring at him. I somehow finally managed to whisper a soft "Thank you for the gifts" before a pounding on the window broke the silence. Started, all three of us jumped to see Fireman Bob's goofy grin peering back at us.

"Well, aren't you going to let me in?" he mouthed.

I rose and pushed the window open so Bob could crawl in.

"Hope I'm not interrupting anything," he said.

"Wait a minute," I retorted. "How'd you get up here? We're on the fifth floor."

Shooting my head out the window for an answer, I met the eye of another firefighter who was climbing the same ladder that Bob had obviously used. Looking further down, I saw seven more firefighters following suit. A total of nine firefighters had arrived to pay their fellow brother a visit, and their entrance had given new life and energy to little Bopsy, whose hysterical and infectious laugh would have seemed impossible just a few moments before. They stood around Bopsy's bed, telling jokes and telling stories about their shift the day before. There was no question that Bopsy was loving every minute of it. Being surrounded by his heroes was yet another dream come true.

After shaking Bob's hand, I turned to leave, pausing for just a moment to hug Bopsy one more time.

"I'll see you later," I said.

I never did.

Pancho: Puedo Power la Siren, Frank?

Chapter Seventeen
Building Foundations

The amazing amount of support, contributions, and generosity we'd witnessed while granting Chris and Bopsy's wishes only served to reinforce my belief that our foundation had a future. Kitty, too, was fully dedicated to our organization and its purpose, but Linda had doubts. Sure, she'd witnessed what we'd been able to do and the fact that we really did make a difference in the lives of her son and Bopsy. She didn't doubt our purpose but rather our ability to sustain our cause and continue to receive support and funding from people one, five, or ten years down the road.

I, on the other hand, maintained my conviction. "I really believe it. I really believe that this foundation will one day help children all over the world."

Of course, the real test was time.

While that time elapsed, there were many changes in my life. While working together on the foundation, Kitty and I grew closer and eventually began dating. Actually, by that any lights or sirens to signify that I was a police officer, but somehow I needed to get through the traffic so I could assist the victims. Using a little ingenuity, I laid on the horn and held my badge out the window, hoping that it would encourage some drivers to let me through. Then I pulled out my portable police radio, which I always carried on me, and shouted into its microphone.

"Phoenix, Motor 1091!"

"Motor 1091," dispatch responded.

"I'm off duty in civilian clothes, arriving at a multiple vehicle 962, with all northbound lanes blocked. My location is I-17, just north of the New River on-ramp. I need several rescue units. Two of the vehicles are rollovers, and several victims have been ejected."

"Motor 1091, 10-4. A marked vehicle is 10-19 (en route) and should arrive at the scene within minutes," the dispatcher replied with a calm composure that I didn't possess at that moment.

"I'll stay at the scene to assist," I replied.

Finally managing to squeeze through the traffic and make my way across the highway, I reasoned that I was as close as I was going to get and ran over to the accident. In front of me was an officer who had just arrived on the scene. As I approached, he didn't acknowledge me—he just stood there, seemingly paralyzed, with his eyes glued to the scene in front of him.

Even for a seasoned officer like me, it was overwhelming.

Bodies, ripped and strewn on the desert floor, lay motionless in the dirt. They were as still as the officer, until I gripped his shoulder and placed my badge in front of his eyes. When he turned toward me, I recognized him as a recent graduate of the police academy and knew what was happening. He was inexperienced and in shock at the gruesome scene. It became readily apparent that I would have to take charge, and quickly. I started shouting orders and was grateful that he'd pulled himself together enough to respond to every command I sent his way, the first of which was to administer first aid to the victims on the ground.

A quick evaluation of the scene didn't give me the answers I was seeking. *Who needs me most? Who do I help first?* Those answers don't come when at first glance every victim appears to be fighting for his life.

So I did the only thing I could. In training, we're taught not to waste time asking questions in situations like this. Instead, we're told to act. Every second counts. The first victim was a frail older woman who was lying on her back. She choked, then gasped for air, and I could see she was failing. Grabbing her face, I pinched her nose closed and placed my lips over mouth and exhaled. Her chest rose, but her response was slow. As I conducted CPR, she faded in and out of consciousness, barely hanging on, but I could tell that she was not breathing on her own. I pounded on her chest and again breathed into her mouth, providing her with enough air to keep her alive for just a few seconds, before I repeated the process again. That's what I was doing when the dispatcher summoned me.

"Motor 1091, I have an urgent message for you. I need you to leave the accident and get to a payphone."

Knowing that leaving the woman would result in her death, I ignored the communication and continued administering CPR to the woman. The sounds of a chopper overhead provided me with welcome relief—help had arrived. Looking around, I noticed that the scene was now swarming with officers, paramedics, and firefighters. At this point, an officer I knew approached me and shouted in order to be heard over the deafening sounds of the helicopters.

"I'll take over here. You need to leave and get to a payphone and call dispatch. They have an urgent message for you," he shouted.

"What's going on?" I asked, reluctant to leave the scene.

"Just go," he replied. "We have everything under control."

As told, I got back in my Bronco and drove to the nearest payphone. It was then that I learned that my father had passed away.

I hadn't seen my father for several years. The last time I had seen him, he looked great. He had battled alcohol problems and had gone through a separation with my stepmother, but he had gone into rehab and managed to salvage his marriage. We had a great time during our visit; Dad's sense of humor shone, and the evening was full of fun and laughter and my stepmother's famous fried chicken, which

I'd always loved. I'm grateful that we had a chance to share a private moment, and I'll always cherish the words that he told me that night. It meant so much to me to hear him say how proud he was of me for serving in the Air Force, and especially proud that I was a motorcycle officer with the highway patrol. There hadn't been much publicity about Chris and what we had done for him, but nonetheless, Dad listened and expressed his approval.

For some children, a parent's approval might be taken for granted, but not for me. Because my father and I had lived apart and in different areas of the country, our conversations were limited. Our visitations were even fewer. Time and opportunity had never opened themselves up to allow us to have such a personal conversation, especially as adults. These are words that most children need to hear from their parents, and I was no exception. The fact that I had made my dad proud meant the world to me.

It was Kitty who held and consoled me as I grieved my father's death. It was Kitty who stayed by my side when I scattered his ashes from a helicopter over a mountain range in Arizona. It was Kitty who refused to leave my side when I was once again injured while on duty.

It was 1982, and I was training a cadet car officer. A drunk driver pursuit took us off the highway and into Phoenix's city streets. I was the passenger and was observing the cadet who was driving to make sure she followed procedures. Lights and sirens activated, we approached an intersection, and the light had turned red. After making sure other cars had the opportunity to see us, we pulled into the intersection and were struck by a speeding car, with the impact occurring on the passenger side. I was trapped in the vehicle with the crushed pillar of the door on my head. Unconscious, I had to be cut out of the vehicle by emergency personnel.

My cadet called in the accident, stating that there was a 962A (an officer injured in an accident). When my sergeant heard the transmission, he went into Kitty's office and, somehow, they managed to be there before the ambulance arrived. As they wheeled me into the emergency room, they ordered Kitty to leave, but she refused. Instead, she gave them a rundown of my past injuries, stating that I had suffered a skull fracture in the past as well as two previous concussions from accidents that occurred while I was on duty.

When I regained consciousness, the first thing I saw was her smile.

Kitty did everything she could to help me through my recovery. I had suffered another skull fracture and a severely bruised brain. As a result, I struggled to do even the most minor tasks. I couldn't focus or tell left from right, and had to relearn how to do just about everything, from cooking to cleaning. I had even forgotten tasks as simple as opening cans.

Because Kitty had to work, she couldn't stay with me day

and night. So she made arrangements for my stepmother, Elinor, to come to Arizona and help. It hadn't occurred to me to ask her for assistance, mostly because when Kitty mentioned her, I couldn't remember who she was. Kitty made the call, anyway, and because we'd always been fond of each other, and my stepmother was alone after my father's death, she was happy to come to Arizona and take care of me.

I have to admit that there wasn't any one thing that made me love Kitty—it seemed that everything she did endeared her to me a little more. However, there were several things that occurred that told she was "the one." First, my two young daughters liked her immediately, and I cannot overemphasize how important that was to me. To this day, they are very close, just like I have always been with my stepmother.

The second thing that happened caught me off guard. Kitty had never done much traveling during her life, so when I was planning to visit one of my vacation areas, I asked her to join me. We would take my motorcycle for a two-week camping trip to the Grand Teton/Yellowstone area in Wyoming. Many women would balk at the idea of spending three days riding a motorcycle, camping each night, enduring cold weather, and eating less-than-impressive meals, but not Kitty. She was a real trooper. Still, I didn't know she was my life and soul mate until, as the mountain range came into view on one really cold morning, she asked me to pull over. I watched as she got off the bike and removed her helmet, and I was surprised to see that she was crying. Before I could ask her what was wrong, she spoke these words: "It's so beautiful, purple mountains majesty, thank you." It was then, at that very second, that I knew I would never let her go.

While vacationing in the Grand Canyon, I finally asked Kitty Carlisle to marry me. We married in 1983, the same year that the Make-A-Wish Foundation went national.

Chapter Eighteen
Wish Legacy

It took three years after granting Bopsy's wish for the Foundation to go national, but our efforts paid off. We continued raising money and granting wishes, and as we did, we gained the increased support of local businesses, corporations, fundraisers, individuals, and volunteers. As our cause gained support, interest, and exposure, branches began to sprout in every state. After ten more years, Make-A-Wish became an international foundation and was granting wishes to children across the globe.

I continued to work as a highway patrol officer and was eventually promoted to detective. I still spent a great deal of time on the foundation, but over the years, my involvement transitioned. We'd come a long way from our funding days and granting our first wish to Bopsy, and with our growth, my role became a smaller one. I was the first official president, but there were so many people now serving these children and their families that I was able to contribute in a different way. As a wish ambassador for the national office, located in Phoenix, Arizona, I have had the pleasure and privilege of being able to travel and share our story with so many. It was during one such trip that I learned just how important our foundation had actually become.

Twenty years after granting Bopsy's wish, the national office asked me to travel to Saipan and Guam, where I would represent them at a few speaking engagements and galas. The plane ride was long, and I was more than ready to depart when we landed. Joining my fellow passengers who were waiting for the doors to open, I rested my arm against the back of a seat so I could slouch just enough to keep my tall frame from hitting the ceiling.

Ahead of me, I heard a man say "excuse me" a few times, and as the people moved to the side, I noticed two uniformed officers walking down the aisle.

"Are you Frank Shankwitz?" one asked.

"Yes, that's me. What's going on?"

"Please come with us," was their only answer. I followed them back to the doors, realizing we were cutting in front of other people who were also waiting to exit the plane. Feeling guilty, I muttered "excuse me" several times, hoping they would forgive us for our lack of courtesy. Then I followed the officers in silence, which was broken the moment we stepped into the airport.

Cameras flashed from every direction, and questions came from even more. "Mr. Shankwitz, may we have a few words with you?" "How long will you be on the island?" "What are your plans while you're here?"

I was flabbergasted. It was the first, and only, time I'd ever been treated like a celebrity. Composing myself, I attempted to answer the questions that were being thrown at me from left and right, until they felt they had what they needed to write their stories.

The officers had been standing on the sideline, waiting patiently.

"Frank, we would like you to meet Pete Tenorio, the governor of Saipan, and his wife, Sophie," one said.

Wearing a Hawaiian shirt, the governor shot me a bright smile. While I should have been impressed at being fortunate enough to personally meet the governor of the beautiful island, it was he who seemed excited to meet me. Extending his arm, he shook my hand and with a broad smile said, "I'm so glad to meet you, Mr. Shankwitz."

"The pleasure is all mine, Governor Tenorio," I replied, adding, "and you can call me Frank."

"Call me Pete," he nodded, then looked toward his wife.

"And you can call me Sophie. We welcome you to the island."

More than a little shocked at my reception, I retrieved my luggage from baggage claim and then followed Pete and Sophie outside to their shiny black limousine.

"The driver will put your things in the trunk," Pete advised. "Climb inside."

Sitting in the back of the limousine, I turned to what I was beginning to believe were my hosts and asked them where we were going.

"To the Hyatt Regency Resort, where you'll be staying," Pete indicated. "Would you like to join us for dinner?"

Despite the jet lag that was quickly catching up with me, I found myself accepting the invitation . . . and glad that I did.

A group of people were waiting in the hotel restaurant when we arrived, and I found myself surrounded by Make-A-Wish volunteers, sponsors, and retired governors. Introductions were made and many hands were shaken before we made our way to the buffet line. We talked for couple hours over a delicious meal of fish, rice, bread, fruit, and Spam—yes, Spam, but not just any Spam—Spam with bacon, hot and spicy Spam, and honey Spam—not because it was delicacy, but rather because it served as a humble reminder of post World War II, when the United States Marines liberated the island and brought cans of Spam to the people to feed them. Their respect for this patriotic and humanitarian gesture was touching.

The rest of the week was well spent. I spoke at various functions about Make-A-Wish, while raising both money and awareness about our mission. On a social note, I had the pleasure of playing golf and fishing with various CEOs and businesspeople, as well. I even had some spare time to partake in one of my favorite pastimes, visiting historic battle sites and ruins, like I had done so many years before when I was stationed in London. Sophie, the governor's wife, even commented on my interest, stating that she felt it was wonderful.

My official host during my stay was a gentleman named David Sablan, who was a member of the board of directors of the Northern Mariana Islands Make-A-Wish chapter, which covered the islands of Saipan, Guam, and Tinian. It just so happened that Guam was the next destination on our agenda.

When the plane landed in Guam, two policemen walked down the aisle and asked if I was Frank Shankwitz. Again, I stated that I was he, and the ritual that we followed in Saipan was repeated. Again, I was met by a governor, Carl Gutierrez, who was the governor of Guam, and another round of television and newspaper reporters. After answering their questions and smiling for the cameras, I had an opportunity to speak with the governor, who informed me that I would be staying at the governor's mansion.

I was shocked and more than a little impressed. The Make-A-Wish Foundation and the hosts on these islands had surpassed all of my expectations, a fact that was reinforced when I saw that the limousine awaiting my arrival had a motorcycle escort.

"I should be the guy leading this, not sitting in the limo," I pointed out to the driver as he opened the back door.

The governor and I had a nice talk while en route to his mansion, situated beautifully at the peak of a hill that overlooked the entire city of Agana. The mansion itself was quite modest; however, the grounds were a spectacular display of nature's glory. An abundance of jungle trees topped the scene, while vivid tropical flowers bloomed vibrantly below. The island's beauty was both remarkable and memorable, and between speaking engagements and sightseeing tours, I was able to experience even more of its beauty and history. I even managed to visit some World War II memorial sites and battlegrounds thanks to my host, Ed Camacho.

It was Ed who came into my room two nights before I was scheduled to leave to tell me, "Your schedule has been so busy, we feel you need to take the day off tomorrow."

When I asked him who "we" was, he stated it included him and some local Make-A-Wish children.

"May we pick you up tomorrow morning at eight thirty?" he asked.

"Sure," I agreed, wondering just what tomorrow held in store.

The next morning, I walked outside to find four parked cars and at least fifteen people standing around them. I couldn't help but notice that all eyes were on me as I approached.

Right then, Ed stepped forward.

"Good morning, Frank." He then proceeded to introduce me to ten Make-A-Wish kids and their mothers before advising that he was sending me off with them for the day.

Crawling into one car full of a few kids and their moms, I couldn't help but feel overwhelmed by all of this unexpected attention. But more than anything, my curiosity was piqued wondering just where we were going as the car maneuvered its way through the rainforest, bouncing on dirt roads. I turned to the kids and asked where they were taking me, but they weren't talking—it was a surprise.

When the car stopped in a clearing, I was even more puzzled. From all appearances, we had parked in an isolated spot that could best be described as the middle of nowhere. But before I could ask what was going on, I heard a loud and unusual noise not far off in the distance. Turning my head its way, I saw what resembled a tank but sounded more like a tractor. Headed toward us was a World War II army deuce-and-a-half truck. My confusion level soared.

"Okay, kids, get up there," yelled one of the moms. Smiling, she then turned to me and said, "You, too."

I followed orders and sat in the back of the truck among all ten kids and their mothers, obviously the only one who had no idea what was going on. The truck jerked and sprang into action, taking us on a path into the thick of the trees. Finally, we rounded a corner, and my eyes took in a beautiful sight—the bluest expanse of sea I'd ever seen. Still, we didn't stop. The truck trudged on, its tires teasing the water's edge before they eventually were knee high in water. It effortlessly rolled over rocks and manipulated the sea's terrain without faltering. The kids found it to be an adventure, giggling in delight with each bounce and sway. Not only were they enjoying the trip, but they also managed to inject their curiosity between bouts of laughter.

"How tall are you, Frank?"

"Are you a giant?"

Smiling, I assured them that I was, in fact, human.

"I'm six foot two."

"Ooooh, you're tall!" Their response was unanimous and spoken in unison.

"Here we are," the driver announced as he parked the military beast on the whitest sand and the most breathtaking beach I'd ever seen. A handmade wooden sign posted nearby marked our destination—Jinapsan Beach.

The reflection of light from the sun and water danced like tiny diamonds in the sand as small waves of water pushed onto the shore, marking their visit with a curved ridge of white foam as they were swallowed back up by the sea. Above us, the tops of the palm trees swayed gently to and fro in the gentle breeze. In the distance below were several thatched huts. It was a glimpse of the island that I hadn't yet seen, and one that would remain ingrained in my mind for the rest of my life.

"C'mon, Frank!" While partaking of the beauty of the surroundings, the kids had circled me. Not shy, they reached for my hands and tugged at my shirt. They were ready to play, and it was obvious that they expected me to, as well.

"Let Frank relax today," one of the mothers insisted. Putting the ball in my court, she asked, "Frank, what would you like to do to relax?"

I looked at the kids, all ranging in age from seven to ten, and could see the expectation in their eyes. There was no way I could deny them. In fact, I didn't want to. I was ready.

"Actually, I'd like to get in the ocean," I said to a roar of cheers.

They had come prepared. Suddenly, the beach was covered with Frisbees, red, blue, and yellow beach balls, and other water toys. Playfully, I rose and, surrounded by ten jubilant kids, ran into the ocean, where we spent the next two hours splashing and enjoying the water, throwing Frisbees and using our architectural skills to make sand castles.

Then, two of the children grabbed my hands and pulled me toward the shore.

"What's the matter?"

"There are jellyfish in the water," one said. "Let's go see the rainforest."

After announcing where we were going, we were joined by the rest of the kids and a few of their mothers. The kids took the opportunity to give me a little education.

"If you hear a rustle in the leaves, that probably means a coconut is falling, so watch out," one of the older kids warned.

As though on command, a coconut fell from above,

landing just a few feet in front of us. Laughing hysterically, the timing wasn't lost on the children.

Our walk through the rainforest was enjoyable, but hot. The humidity was thick, and the air became heavier and hotter where the sun's rays managed to seep through an opening in the trees. Occasionally, the kids would stop to point out something interesting, teaching me about the bounty of the rainforest. Our walk was punctuated by lively conversation, and I was enjoying it just as much as the kids.

Suddenly, though, they grew quiet. Ahead of us was pack of wild boars. One of the kids whispered, "Don't walk toward them. Just walk to the side."

Cautiously and silently I followed their lead, and we moved past the pigs without incident. Then, one of the mothers suggested that we head back to the beach.

Following the same trail, we eventually came back to the clearing, where, to my surprise, we were greeted by three large tables covered with food. It looked like a party.

"What's this?" I asked.

"It's a surprise luau!" the kids yelled as they sauntered into a run. Catching their excitement, I sped up my pace, as well, finding that running through the thick sand wasn't as easy as I had thought.

Trying to catch my breath, I sat down in a wooden chair. Suddenly, the kids bolted into action. Scrambling to and fro, they vied for the chance to grab a plateful of food and bring it to me. I didn't have to move a muscle. Then, when they were satisfied that I had enough roast pork, beef, and fruit, they filled their own plates and sat down to eat.

Rising to get a glass of tea, I was interrupted by a young boy.

"Sit down, Frank," he said. "What can I get you?"

"Uh, I was just going to get some tea."

"I'll get it for you," he said and was off like a bullet to do just that.

A little girl then walked over to me. Unfolding a paper napkin, she sweetly tucked it into the top of my shirt. "There, you might need that." She smiled.

I was taken aback, realizing that these children, these kids who at one time were close to dying and needed someone to take care of them and their needs, were now waiting on me. Hand and foot, they anticipated my every need and refused to let me lift a finger.

To say I was touched would be an understatement of the greatest proportions. Pursing my lips together was unsuccessful, so I had to use my hand to cover my quivering chin. When I realized that controlling the tears that threatened to fall was a lost cause, I silently stood and walked toward the ocean. Lighting a cigar in an effort to regain my composure, I looked out at the vast sea and contemplated what had just happened. But most of all, I soaked it all in. Standing on the sunny shore, I felt the love flow through me as I listened to the laughter and banter of the kids behind me. So full of life, so full of joy, no one would have ever guessed that they once fought for their lives. And they survived, stronger and braver. They were as generous and unselfish and giving as the day was long, and through their generosity, kindness, and love, I was experiencing one of the most defining moments of my life.

That day, ten children touched my soul at the barest and deepest level. They had been given another chance at life, and they lived it with zest and gratitude. That day, I knew without a glimmer of doubt just why I had been given a second chance at life. Through them, my purpose had been reinforced.

Dr. Frank & Mrs. Kathleen Carlisle Shankwitz

Chapter Nineteen
350,000 Wishes

In 2014, I hung up my badge and retired from the police force. It had been a good run, a long and rewarding career that gave me an opportunity to serve others. Throughout my career, I met wonderful people, including my partners and fellow officers. To this day, we share an unbreakable bond and an even deeper respect. Through the good and the bad, I would do it all over again.

Yes, I suffered serious injuries. Yes, I actually died once. My career as a police officer made me question my existence. Why am I here? Why was I given a second chance? Not knowing the answers to life's most profound questions made me feel lost and vulnerable, but I had faith—faith that the answers would come someday.

Then I met Chris, a sweet and energetic boy who somehow managed to be bursting with life even as his was ending. Accepting the request to help him quickly turned into a desire to do more for the little seven-year-old boy who instantly found a place within my heart and made it grow beyond any expectation.

Losing Chris was heartbreaking, but I knew that his life also had a purpose. We had come together for a reason, though I wasn't sure just what it was. I listened to my soul, which continually led me right back to my heart, where the answer had always been. Because of Chris, I learned a valuable life lesson—when something or someone touches you that deeply, to the core of your being and the depths of your heart, there is always a reason. When you become so passionate about something that it consumes you, you've found your purpose. Listen carefully; it's there, just waiting for you to finally discover it.

Because of Chris, my whole life changed. And then I met Bopsy, the bravest little Pancho I'll ever know. Two sweet and loving seven-year-old boys changed my life and, as a result, the lives of children all across the world.

Why me? Why did these boys come into my life and inspire the largest not-for-profit foundation for children that ever existed? It's been said that accidents happen for reason. I now know why I was in that fatal accident but survived. It was for kids like Chris and Bopsy, who deserve so much more than we can give them. As a child, I didn't have much, but through my dear friend, Juan, I learned that even when we don't think we have anything to give, we do.

The Make-A-Wish Foundation has come a long way

from the days when we sat across a kitchen table drafting bylaws and granting our first wish. I'm proud to say that thirty-five years later, the organization has granted wishes to more than 350,000 children and counting. Today, Kitty and I are privileged to travel and spread awareness about the foundation, but most of all the children. For it is their stories, not mine, that serve as our inspiration, touch us at the deepest levels, and show us the real meaning of life and love.

I am proud to be affiliated with the Make-A-Wish Foundation and every child it has served. Through them, my life's journey has been enriched, and I wake up every day with a passion to make a difference in their lives. It was once enough for me to be a dad, a cowboy, and a highway patrol officer. But my destination changed. I didn't know I wanted to be here, but I know it is precisely where I am supposed to be.

About the Author

Frank Shankwitz is best known as the creator and a founder of the Make-A-Wish Foundation, an extraordinary charity that grants wishes to children with life threatening illnesses. From humble beginnings, the Make-A-Wish Foundation has grown to a global organization that grants a child's wish somewhere in the world on average every 28 minutes of the day. Frank is a U.S. Air Force veteran and has a long and distinguished career in law enforcement. He began as an Arizona Highway Patrol Motorcycle Officer, and retired as a Homicide Detective with the Arizona Department of Public Safely with 42 years of service. Frank has been featured in numerous publications and television shows and has received several awards, including the White House Call to Service Award from President George W. Bush. In 2015, Frank joined six U.S. Presidents, as well as Nobel Prize winners and industry leaders, as a recipient of the Ellis Island Medal of Honor. In December 2015, Frank was a presented with an Honorary Doctorate Degree, Doctor of Public Service, from The Ohio State University. On December 30, 2015, Frank was identified as one of the "10 Most Amazing Arizonians" in a front-page article in the Arizona Republic newspaper. On January 5, 2016, Frank was identified in a Forbes Magazine article as a Top Ten Keynote Speaker. Frank's life story will soon be featured in the upcoming independent motion picture, "Wish Man." Further information is available on Frank's website at www.wishman1.com.